FLESH & BLOOD

by

JOHN ARGUS

CHIMERA

Flesh & Blood first published in 2004 by
Chimera Publishing Ltd
PO Box 152
Waterlooville
Hants
PO8 9FS

Printed and bound in Great Britain by
Cox & Wyman Ltd, Reading.

The characters and situations in this book are entirely imaginary and bear no relation to any real person or actual happening.

FLESH & BLOOD

John Argus

This novel is fiction – in real life practice safe sex

'The pleasure is unfeigned. This is the moment of glory, the moment when the skin flashes fire, when the body writhes and the world explodes within her. That is what I seek to capture on canvas.'

'How do you know she's not faking it?' Leah asked, driven by her own alarming curiosity. He turned those dark eyes on her and smiled, and she felt her legs tremble and her stomach flutter.

'I know,' he said assuredly.

'But… but how could you?' she couldn't help but ask.

'Allow me.' His fingers slipped beneath the edges of her blazer and pulled it back over her shoulders.

'I…I don't…' she stammered, but without thinking she drew her arms back, allowing him to remove the garment.

'Shhh,' he cajoled, then drew her forward between a pair of waist high posts. Each had a brass ring at its top, and a thin chain attached. He drew her right arm out to one side and attached a shackle to it. Leah felt her stomach lurch and opened her mouth to protest; yet no sound emerged.

Chapter One

The car pulled to the curb and Scott yawned, covering his mouth briefly, then turned and grinned at her. 'Odds or evens?'

Leah shrugged, reaching into her purse for her badge, then pinning it to the pocket of her blazer. The two climbed out of the unmarked car and separated, Scott crossing the road while Leah moved to the nearest home on the block, clipboard in hand.

It was extremely unlikely any individual along this street would have anything to contribute to their search. It was unlikely, in fact, that any of them would have much of interest to the police investigation. Still, it was a time-honored method of gathering information. It had to be done. She just wished she hadn't been delegated to do it.

It was a well-heeled neighborhood, home to an unfortunate number of seniors who, in Leah's experience, found it thrilling to speak to the police and tried to extend the event as far as possible.

The first house was home to a dignified, pipe-smoking gentleman and his overweight wife, both of whom spent far more time trying to get information out of her than trying to facilitate her own investigation. The second was worse; an elderly widow who insisted on feeding her scones and chatting on about her neighbors' foibles, her grandchildren, and the lack of morality of young girls today.

As the investigation concerned the disappearances, likely

by foul play, of several young women, Leah found it difficult to keep from expressing her irritation. She wondered how Mrs Peabody would react if she had arrived in one of her short skirts or tight tops, both of which were mentioned frequently in her headshaking analyses of the reasons men were tempted by immoral young females.

She did, however, have one bit of information Leah filed away for action: a suspicious neighbour. Oh, it was normal enough for a woman like Mrs Peabody to be suspicious of almost anyone different, especially a foreigner, but there was an odd catch to the woman's lowered voice, a quiver almost of actual fear, as she mentioned Mr Morales.

Mr Morales apparently lived two houses down, and was quite 'suspicious'. Oddly, Mrs Peabody, who'd lived in the same home for several decades, could not say how long Mr Morales had lived in his. She seemed under the impression he had always been there, though she described him as a 'young man'.

The next house over produced a family of five. Two of the children were teenage girls, which produced the anticipated high level of helpful interest in their parents. However, they had nothing of substance to add to the information Leah already had.

The next home was Mr Morales'. It was a large, but unremarkable gray stone house with a sloping black tile roof. Chimneys pushed through at either end, and half a dozen windows looked down from the first floor onto a large front yard. Tall hedges and trees shadowed the yard itself, but the lawn was well maintained, the path to the front door swept.

Yet despite a low level of confidence in Mrs Peabody's concerns, she found herself looking a little nervously about as she walked through the darkened yard. The branches overhead swayed creakily with a stiff chill wind swirling through their leaves, and the shadows seemed to dance and roll along the ground as she walked through them. They played upon the flat gray stone with an almost sinister air, and she licked her lips and clutched her blazer a little tighter around herself as she climbed the steps to the front porch.

The impact of her knuckles was so minimal she realized at once the door was heavy and solid, not the hollow frame construction one normally encountered. There was no bell so she used the heavy brass knocker, hammering it firmly against the plate beneath.

She was a police officer, and this was a routine interview in search of information. While it was true one of the missing girls lived nearby, there was nothing whatever that indicated her suspect or suspects lived in this area. It was, in fact, quite unlikely.

A sound made her whirl suddenly, a chill running up her spine as her eyes tried to pierce the darker shadows, but though she saw nothing she felt her heart beating more quickly.

'Yes?'

The almost sibilant whisper made her gasp and swing round towards the door again. A very tall man in a dark suit stood there, bald, his face long and emotionless. His eyes were so deep-set within his angular face they were almost lost in the shadows. Leah took a deep breath to steady herself, cursing softly under her breath at Mrs Peabody. 'Mr Morales?' she asked.

'I am his manservant,' the man said, in a voice so quiet she had to strain to hear.

'I'm Detective Leah MacInnes. I'd like to speak to Mr Morales, please.'

The man stared at her for a long moment, and Leah felt

both rising annoyance and a sense of discomfort under his blank gaze. Why, she wondered, hadn't Mrs Peabody mentioned this man? Surely the sight of him would rouse considerably more doubt than the owner himself.

'One moment,' he said.

He closed the door in her face, and Leah glared at it even while feeling a sense of relief. 'Shit,' she whispered, rubbing her arms and again glancing about.

The door opened a long minute later and the man stepped back, revealing a narrow hall, a chandelier hanging just within. 'Mr Morales will see you,' he said.

Leah stepped inside, feeling her soft leather shoes sink into the deep red carpet that ran the length of the hall. She turned quickly to face the man as he closed the door, not wanting him behind her, and then followed as he wordlessly led her deeper into the gloomy house.

There were closed doors on either side of her, and to the left the same blood-red carpet rose up a wide staircase with an ornately carved wooden banister.

They turned into a capacious living room, heavy red velvet curtains covering the front windows to her right, a fire flickering in an immense marble hearth to her left. The furniture was heavy leather and dark-grained wood, probably not antique, but quite old-fashioned nonetheless.

Aside from the fireplace, the only light in the dimly lit room came from a pair of lamps in a corner near the window, and a large man sat comfortably in a chair before the fireplace. The chair itself had a very high back and arms that served to keep him in shadow as Leah moved to him.

'Mr Morales?' she asked.

She reached to shake hands almost automatically, regretting it the instant she saw his pale hand rise to clasp hers. It was icy cold, yet large and powerful, and she gasped, feeling a strange shock run through her as they made contact. She felt her legs grow weak and sank down onto a pillowed ottoman just in front of the chair. 'I, um, I would, that is, I'm with the Los Angeles Police,' she said, her voice quivering strangely. She cleared her throat in annoyance with herself, and shook her head so that her brown hair swirled around her shoulders. 'I wonder if we could have more light, sir,' she said.

'Why, I wonder, do people avoid the dark so?' he asked rhetorically, his voice a bass rumble with a thick Spanish accent. 'Is it that their own fears can take form in the darkness?' He reached out to switch on a lamp on the side table by his chair, and the shadows created by the soft yellow glow of the fire and the lamp now diminished enough to make out his features, yet the room was scarcely much brighter.

He was in his mid-forties, she thought, creepily handsome, with thick, shaggy hair spilling down in loose curls around his head. He had a square face with a firm jaw and wide, full lips. His eyes were so darkly brown as to be almost black.

'What was your name?'

'Detective MacInnes,' she said, unaccountably nervous.

'Your first name.'

It occurred to tell him that should be of little concern, but being polite with potential witnesses seldom did any harm. 'Leah.'

'Leah,' he said, rolling out the word in his deep, low voice. 'A lovely name, Leah.'

'Thank you,' she said, producing a wan smile. 'I wonder, Mr Morales, if you are aware of the investigation into missing girls taking place. It's been somewhat in the media the last few weeks.'

'I do not read the newspapers,' he said. 'And I have no

television.'

'Well, er, three girls—'

'Children?'

'Well, no, young women.'

'Ah,' he said, his head nodding. 'The prey in the game of life.'

She blinked at him. 'Prey?'

He smiled, and she felt a strange glow within her belly, which sank through her abdomen.

'Aren't all attractive young women prey to the animal hungers of men?'

'In a manner of speaking,' she said. 'But many would say the reverse is true, as well.'

He chuckled throatily, and she felt a tightness in her chest. 'Young women seek a man to protect them, to support them, to father children by them. Young men seek women to conquer, to use, to satisfy their lusts, to prove their virility upon their bodies. Surely you are aware of this. You are a sexually desirable young female. You look to have a healthy body beneath those masculine clothes. Your breasts appear full and your hips well rounded.'

She felt blood rush to her face. 'We should speak about the issue at hand, please,' she said. Yet that warm glow in her abdomen spread lower still, and she subconsciously squeezed her thighs together, feeling a moist heaviness sink into her loins.

'I thought we were,' he said, his voice somber yet melodic. 'What do you believe has happened to these young women?'

'That is what we are investigating,' she said.

'But you have your suspicions,' he said softly. 'Suspicions that these young does have been brought down by some hungry wolf, their bodies a feast for his lust.'

'This is a serious investigation, Mr Morales,' she said

sternly.

'Of course it is. The veneer of civilization is thin upon us all. We are predators, we men, and all our instincts, upon seeing an unattached female in the full bloom of her breeding season, is to bring her to her knees and mount her.'

He leaned forward slightly and she felt her eyes caught by his, felt something within her twist and crumble. The moist heaviness in her loins began to seep outward and she felt a heat rising within her body. Her nipples tightened within the cups of her bra, and she felt a sense of confusion and disbelief at the sense of arousal growing within her.

'I'm sure you've felt it yourself many times,' he said, his voice almost hypnotic, 'the lust of the men around you, their eyes crawling over your body, the hunger in their words as they seek to persuade you to shed your clothes and inhibitions and join them in the ancient dance of flesh.'

'You have such an optimistic view of humanity,' she said sarcastically, fighting to keep her composure even as her heart pounded.

He smiled again, almost tolerantly... or was it contemptuously? She felt her pulse race a little and straightened her shoulders, pushing her breasts out more firmly against the thin fabric of her blouse.

'What, um, w-what do you do for a living, Mr Morales?' she asked, increasingly flustered.

'I am an artist.'

The corners of his lips turned up again, and Leah pressed the tip of her pen against her pad to help keep her hand from shaking. He reached out to the table beside him and lifted a crystal wine glass to his lips, sipping lightly. His movements were graceful and fluid, and she found herself staring in admiration as he set the glass down once again.

'I specialize in the female form,' he said, sitting deeper in the chair. 'Nothing in life is so beautiful. No artist could create a form so perfect.'

Leah reached up to brush aside the chestnut fringe that had spilled across her forehead. She felt very warm and glanced at the flames flickering in the fireplace to her left. Her eyes lifted to the mantle above, and a large painting of a girl. She was nude, backed against a tall post, her arms chained above her head, her back arched, perfect breasts thrust up and out. 'Y-you paint nudes,' she gasped. His lips turned up again and she felt herself melting, her sex thrumming. Confusion twisted through her mind. Why was she so aroused? What on earth was she doing? She ought to be asking...

'I try to capture the female form in its most erotic moments,' he elaborated. 'Come, let me show you.'

He stood up and she half stumbled to her feet, a little dazed as he took her arm and led her from the front room and down a side hall to a back room, bright with track lighting coming from above. There were no windows, which she found surprising, having heard that artists craved natural light. The room was largely unfurnished, but a number of canvases, completed and empty, were propped against the walls. An easel stood in the centre of the room and a large, almost finished painting sat upon it. It was of another naked woman, reclined on a bed, wrists bound to the posts above her head, back arching, legs spread wide, mouth open in a cry. Up and down either side of the easel were black and white snapshots, clearly the woman in the painting, all of them showing her in almost the same pose.

'These were taken as she climaxed,' he said to her wide-eyed, questioning look.

'Uhm, oh,' she gulped, face reddening.

'The pleasure is unfeigned. This is the moment of glory, the moment when the skin flashes fire, when the body writhes and the world explodes within her. That is what I seek to capture on canvas.'

'How do you know she's not faking it?' Leah asked, driven by her own alarming curiosity. He turned those dark eyes on her and smiled, and she felt her legs tremble and her stomach flutter.

'I know,' he said assuredly.

'But... but how could you?' she couldn't help but ask.

'Allow me.' His fingers slipped beneath the edges of her blazer and pulled it back over her shoulders.

'I...I don't...' she stammered, but without thinking she drew her arms back, allowing him to remove the garment.

'Shhh,' he cajoled, then drew her forward between a pair of waist high posts. Each had a brass ring at its top, and a thin chain attached. He drew her right arm out to one side and attached a shackle to it. Leah felt her stomach lurch and opened her mouth to protest; yet no sound emerged. She jerked her arm back, but no real conviction was behind it. And then her other wrist was shackled to the opposite post and her heart was beating like a trip hammer as he moved away to one corner, and maneuvered a tall, antique, gold embossed mirror in front of her, cocked at a slight angle. Her reflected eyes were enormous and her expression stricken. She could see the outline of her erect nipples through her thin blouse, and her cheeks began to flush as she became aware of his scrutiny.

'Y-you should... I mean, please release me,' she said, her voice trembling slightly, her arms held out to either side at waist height. The chains were slender but strong, though she'd made no real effort to pull free.

'But of course,' he said, and moved behind her, his

hands grasping hers for a moment. A shock of excitement rippled through her body and she realized she was beginning to perspire with nervous anticipation of his intentions.

His hands slid gracefully up her arms to her shoulders, and his lips brushed the nape of her neck. Leah could not tear her eyes off the mirror as she watched his mouth drift over her throat and up to her earlobe. Her breathing was growing ragged, her breasts rising and falling rapidly as she swayed where she stood.

'Watch,' he whispered, his voice a soft breath in her ear. His powerful hands squeezed her trim waist for a few seconds, then slid up to her front and cupped her breasts and she could not repress a gasp and a shudder of sexual excitement. Her breasts tingled and warmed within his cupped hands, and she felt her heart beginning to race. His body was molding against her back, she felt his groin pressing against her buttocks, and moaned softly as the sexual heat rose increasingly strong within her. This was insane, she knew. Aside from the shock and shame of allowing a total stranger to chain her and touch her so intimately, her professional instincts admonished her severely for being so stupid as to let herself be lured into a potentially dangerous situation. She was a police officer and this was an inexcusable lapse.

His right hand slid down over her churning tummy, and his fingers nimbly popped the catch at the front of her trousers, the timely touch of his lips against her throat causing her to melt again and silencing the protest she knew she should make.

His hand crept down into her trousers, down into her panties, cool fingers instantly finding her wet sex, brushing her clitoris. The intensity of her reaction shocked her, and her hips rocked forward.

'Watch,' he whispered. His teeth bit lightly into the nape of her neck and she shuddered. She felt a finger curving in and up, felt the soft, swollen lips of her sex spread aside as she was penetrated. She rolled her hips again as his finger pushed deeper, and she felt a wave of shame at how wet she was even as she arched her back in helpless pleasure as the fingers cupping her breast pinched and rolled her nipple through her blouse and bra.

He bit more fervently into her throat, his teeth pricking as they clamped onto her smooth flesh. His hand drew up and out of her trousers and she moaned and swayed, then squealed as he wrenched open the front of her blouse, sending buttons popping onto the floor.

'D-don't,' she pleaded, secretly thrilled at his dominant strength, but he contemptuously tore the blouse right down the back from collar to hem, as if it were paper, and the two ragged tatters of material slid off her shoulders and down her trussed arms. Her bra was removed with similar disregard, and then he was somehow before her, his fingers sliding through her hair, pulling her head back as his teeth bit at her mouth, his tongue darting in and out, his lips voracious, and the sexual tension was more powerful than she had ever felt in her life before.

She collapsed into his arms and he bore her downward to her knees, his mouth still upon hers, his breath drawing hers from her overheated lungs, his tongue leading hers in a ritualistic dance. His hands left her hair, gliding up and down her back. Then one squeezed between them and she felt a throbbing nipple caught between a thumb and forefinger. She trembled as they closed against it, rubbing gently, then squeezing, pinching, rolling the nipple until it sparked like a live electrical wire, then pulsed with pain as they clamped vice-like.

'Do you understand yet, Leah?' he whispered. 'Do you

understand yet?'

And then she was alone. Or at least she felt alone. His body was no longer against hers, no longer touching her. She sagged back dazedly, but now she was on her knees her wrists were held up and to each side and helped support her. She moaned wearily, slowly drawing her head up, and saw him rising tall above her, a hand slowly lowering the zipper of his immaculate trousers.

His cock was dark, like him, and beautiful, like him. It rose at an angle even as it emerged from his clothing, swelling and lengthening before her widening eyes as she gasped at its impressive length and girth. He grasped her hair, filling his fists with its silkiness, forcing her head roughly up and back, and then with one calculated thrust of his hips he thrust himself into her vulnerable mouth.

Despite being a strong-willed woman, Leah let him force her jaws almost painfully wide, filling her mouth with his erection, feeling herself dropping into an utterly submissive role which both frightened and exhilarated her. She raised her eyes and met his, felt herself drowning in his stare, and hardly noticed as his stout cock slid deeper into her mouth, probing against the entrance to her throat.

It pushed deeper still, yet she felt no urge to gag, no sense of choking or panic. Her eyes remained locked to his as inch after inch of him stretched her straining lips, moved across her trembling tongue and down into her throat. Then his torso blocked her vision and she felt her forehead pressed against his abdomen, her face against the soft fabric of his trousers.

Her jaw ached, especially as he began to grind his hips back and forth. Yet aside from a desperate sexual heat, a sense of tranquility and serenity filled her too. She could come to no harm with him. He would never hurt her or allow her to be harmed. And even as her head pounded

16

and her lungs burned from lack of oxygen she did not panic, watching instead, with a strange sense of delight, as his glistening shaft forged in and out of her mouth.

He drew out at last and she inhaled deeply, violently, her head falling back as he released her hair, her body swaying, the pull of the chains on her wrists increasing as they kept her from falling.

He was behind her, drawing her trousers down her thighs to her knees. She groaned weakly as her hips were pulled back, her knees pulled out from under her. The trousers slid down her legs and off, and her legs dropped back to the floor. She was almost hanging by her wrists, the pain as the metal dug into them severe, yet it did nothing to distract from the shameful sexual hunger gripping her body and mind.

A part of her psyche fluttered like a desperate butterfly, shocked, horrified, wondering, amazed. But she ignored it, whimpering in pleasure as she felt his hands on her thighs, spreading her legs and drawing them back, lifting her bottom and positioning her on her knees. She was leaning forward, her torso held up only by the shackles gripping her wrists and spreading her arms wide. She felt his cock against her sex, felt the slippery wetness of her juices and the saliva coating him. Then she felt herself opening against the pressure, felt it mounting as he tried to enter her. Perspiration was meandering down between her breasts. Her body was on fire, both from within and without, and her breathing came in sharp gasps and pants.

She winced at the discomfort against her sex, her brow furrowed and her eyes closed as she felt her labia spreading wider than ever before to accept his mighty cock, and when it slid slowly into her slick sheath she wanted to cry out in wonder and exultation… and then she realized she was.

His hands roamed her body as he drove deeper and deeper, beginning to pump, fighting the tightness of her muscles, plowing his way through them as he rode her trembling body.

Leah bucked back against him, gasping, wild-eyed, ignoring the dull pain as she impaled herself. She needed him deep inside her, all of him. Leah MacInnes, renowned for her calm self-assurance and total professionalism, was chained and being fucked by a member of the public she was supposed to be interviewing regarding a serious investigation! It was unthinkable… but it was exquisite, too.

He was too big for her. She felt his rigid shaft utterly filling her, felt the delicious ache as he moved, pulled back, moved forward again. She shuddered with each of his thrusts and trembled with longing. And she was too tight for him. His impressive cock stretched the taut lips of her dripping sex, the blunt nose forcing aside the walls of her cunt as he buried himself in her body.

The peak of her pleasure came when she was absolutely filled with him; so full she ached. Then he would draw back and she would groan in helpless denial as her pussy grasped for him, the muscles in her arms and legs tensed and straining. Then would come the next deep thrust and the next peak, and as he rode her the pace of the fuck increased. His groin slapped against her buttocks and his fingers dug into her flanks as he rutted in and out of her with remorseless power. Her body shuddered violently beneath the savage onslaught and her dazed mind spun in wonder.

She felt his hand moving, and as his cock again embedded itself deep inside her his fingers found her swollen clitoris, and she was in ecstasy. Leah had never known anything like this before. Her body thrashed in its chain bonds, gripped by a shockwave of intense pleasure. Every nerve spasmed and every muscle tensed. Her insides roiled with the violence of the sensory storm screaming through her. Her thoughts shattered. The world fell away. Nothing could exist at the centre of such a storm.

Almost nothing. One thing remained; the determined thrusting of his stiff erection as it drove deep inside her, and the jarring impact of his groin against her bottom, again and again and again. The rest of the universe was a white wall of sensory overload as her nervous system screamed with the task of conveying such shocking pleasure to an already stunned mind.

Leah came to, and knew nothing at first but a dull pull on her wrists. Her head felt heavy, intolerably heavy, and after a long minute she dared open her eyes and gazed down between her own perspiring breasts.

She was lying on the floor; at least her legs and pelvis were. Her wrists were still shackled to the posts, holding her torso up at an angle, her head hanging.

Eventually she raised it, gasping weakly. She had never felt so exhausted, so utterly drained. As awareness returned she felt the many aches gripping her body. Her hands felt numb. Her legs moved feebly, scrabbling on the floor as she sought to get her knees beneath her.

She let out a soft cry as a hand gripped her hair and yanked her head up and back, and she stared into his eyes and then moaned as his mouth met hers in a possessive kiss. He dragged her forward into his arms, his hands sliding down her back to cup her bottom and knead the fleshy cheeks.

His fingers slid between her legs and discomfort flared an instant before the pleasure. She cried out helplessly, an orgasm instantly rippling through her, although nothing

19

like what she had just experienced. This one was the kind of gentle orgasm she enjoyed at home while using her own fingers or favorite vibrator, but still it left her breathless.

He moved to her side, his strong hands gripping her hips and raising her bottom, lifting her to her knees.

'I—' she started, but his hand cracked across her bottom and she gasped at the unexpected and shocking sting.

'Silence,' he said, and she moaned gratefully as his hand caressed her back, down between and across her buttocks.

'But—'

Another crack of his hand on her bottom silenced her, delivering another sting and inducing another gasp. Yet she made no protest, nor thought to.

His fingers slid between her taut buttocks, down to her sex. She trembled as he cupped it, his palm squeezing gently and rhythmically. Another small orgasm made her head loll down again, hanging limp from her shoulders, causing her hips to roll back against him.

'I think,' he stated quietly, 'that I shall keep you.'

Two fingers sank into her sex and began to ease in and out. Comforting pleasure enveloped her and she whimpered gratefully, moving back against him as his other hand slipped beneath her tummy, his fingers skillfully locating her clitoris. She climaxed yet again, sobbing wearily, faintly aware of his throaty chuckle.

Crack!

His open hand slapped her bottom again, jolting her physically and mentally. 'Naughty girl,' he mocked.

Crack!

Leah's back dipped sharply. Again he was rolling her swollen clitoris between thumb and forefinger, driving her mad with the intensity of the pleasure.

Crack!

'Tell me you belong to me, Leah,' he coaxed smoothly, and she gasped for breath, unable to utter a word, her mouth dry.

Crack!

'Tell me, Leah.' The conflicting pain and pleasure induced by the spanking and the clitoral stimulation was continuous and growing more and more intense.

Crack!

'Are you mine?' he coaxed.

'I... I... *please*...' she wailed.

Crack!

'Are you mine?' he persisted relentlessly.

'Yes!'

'Say it, little one.'

'Oh, I'm yours... please.'

'You belong to me?'

'Yes, I belong to you,' she confirmed deliriously, not caring of the consequences of her commitment.

His fingers pressed between her thighs again and she felt herself melting like butter before fire. His other hand began to spank her bottom again, more quickly now, more steadily, punishing her despite her vow of obedience, and she sobbed pitifully as she came yet again.

She drifted back to consciousness a second time to find herself unshackled, lying on her side on the floor with him smiling down at her.

'You had better go,' he said. 'Your colleagues will be looking for you.'

Leah had barely enough time to remember what had happened or where she was before finding herself outside in the darkness on his stoop, naked, the imposing front door closed behind her.

She had to hold the post to keep from falling, so shaky

were her legs, then her uncertain fingers slid down the smooth wood and she knelt, gasping, her head whirling with confusion, her body utterly drained of all energy. She groaned as she slumped back against the rail of the small portico, her trembling fingers moving to her sex.

There were several police cars parked along the street, including Scott's. All were unmarked and empty, the detectives making their way along the houses, carrying out interviews. She could see, just up the street, a suited man standing in the doorway of an old brick house, talking to a woman holding a baby in her arms.

Her fingers gently stroked her moist sex and she shuddered. She felt so sore, so tender, so battered, yet every touch made her moan softly with carnal longing. But her mind was returning to some state of awareness, accompanied by a sense of shock and fear.

She snatched her fingers away, recalling her whereabouts, dismayed with herself. She scrambled with her clothes, tugging her trousers on then pulling her blazer around her shoulders and thrusting her feet into her shoes. She did not see her underwear or blouse, and had no intention of going back to ask for them. Instead she staggered down the path to the sidewalk and then, swaying and weaving, made her way to her car. The chill in the air helped revive her a little, and she felt a rising sense of awe, shock, stunned amazement, and incredulity.

Fortunately in the trunk of the car she found an old white uniform shirt in a bag, probably thrown there some time before to be laundered. With trembling fingers she removed her blazer and pulled on the shirt, and despite it being too big for her she buttoned it up, tucked it in, and slipped her blazer back on over the top.

Scott would notice it missing, she supposed, but would have no idea what had happened to it.

'Shit!' she whispered angrily. If anyone knew, if anyone guessed, if anyone even suspected what she'd just done whilst on duty. Unprofessional did not even begin to describe the conduct she had just engaged in, and aside from being intensely angry with herself for such a serious lapse, she again couldn't believe that on a personal level she had put herself in such a potentially dangerous position. For all she knew the man could have been a serial rapist and she should have known better, particularly bearing in mind the reason for the investigation she was working on.

What had happened? How could it have happened? If she'd had anything to drink she would have been certain he'd drugged her – but she hadn't so she couldn't use that as an excuse.

Her body still felt a kind of aftershock from those impossible climaxes. Not so long before she'd had to test new stun guns with her colleagues, just to know how it felt. After the shock there had been a kind of frazzled afterglow for long minutes, like a physical memory, and that was what she was feeling now, as if she had just been shocked with a kind of high voltage sexual electricity.

Her fingers patted and straightened her hair, trying to bring it into some semblance of order before someone remarked on it. She was Leah MacInnes, always poised, envied and admired by the other policewomen at Chelsea station, but currently she was a trembling mess trying to pull herself together.

The darkness helped a little, and she stood at the back of the group as the other detectives returned and compared notes before Lieutenant Bradfield. Then she got into the car and let Scott drive, speaking as little as possible, staring without seeing out the side window, wondering if there was still a stunned expression on her face.

Chapter Two

'Morning, Leah. Sleep well?'

'Yes, thanks,' she replied, her soft voice containing the slight southern burr which testified to her Georgia roots.

She wore Louis St. Laurent in gray, small gold buttons down the front of the blazer, a green, high-collared silk shirt beneath, drawn closed around her neck, with a silk scarf wrapped around it.

She had been a little shocked, had cringed that morning at the sight of the bruises around the nape of her neck, with neat little bite marks in several places. The collar and scarf hid it all, and the long sleeves of her blouse, combined with a thick watchband and a bracelet, would hide the shackle marks ringing her wrists.

Her suit was businesslike, but still with a definite feminine touch. Her trousers were form fitting, and hugged the near perfection of her rounded bottom, but that would raise no eyebrows for her blazer hid the fact, and all which would be seen were the razor-sharp creases and the turned up hems brushing the surface of the most expensive black leather running shoes she could find. They were so expensive, in fact, they gleamed as if polished, and none of her superiors, not even the fussy Captain Gladwyck, would realize they were anything but the formal dress shoes required of all non-uniformed staff at Lakewood District.

Beneath her stylish suit she wore rather more feminine things than Captain Gladwyck would probably approve of, for he disapproved of women on general principles, at least those who did not know their place, disapproved of young people almost entirely, and had no time whatsoever for anything which smacked, to his deeply religious sensitivities, of indecency.

It was unlikely then, that he would approve of the delicate silk thong she wore. It consisted of little more than a tiny 'V' of purple fabric over her mons, and two thin strings moving diagonally up across her abdomen to curve across her trim hips. A third string slid up between her buttocks, broadened to an even smaller, inverted triangle of fabric at the cleft, and joined the two small waist strings.

Nor would he have been happy at the lacy purple bra made of silk and French lace, so flimsy the sheer half cups strained to contain the thrust of her full young breasts. Such items conveyed sensual femininity and youthful sexuality, but clothing discretely covered them and not even Gladwyck would have had the temerity to demand to examine the underthings of those 'fortunate' to be beneath his supervision.

Leah always liked to dress well, and she always wore sensuous lingerie, even when in uniform. But today she felt much more conscious of it.

She had not slept well at all, taking hours to fall asleep, her mind constantly replaying what had happened, her body reliving it through the helpless stroking of her fingers between her thighs. She had been incredibly horny, nothing like the intensity she felt in Morales' house, but she was unable to keep her hands off her body, and was forced to masturbate three times in an effort to purge her body and mind of sexual hunger.

She tossed and turned in her sleep to dreams of Morales taking her in every conceivable way, to dreams of her prostrating herself before him, worshipping him, adoring him, giving herself to him, submitting herself, body and mind and soul. She awoke again and again; her body inflamed, her sex wet, and masturbated to powerful climaxes. She'd never known a night like it. What was the matter with her?

She turned into the briefing room and found a spot next to Sara Yi, nodding cordially as she slipped her Gucci bag onto the floor next to her chair, then sat down – gingerly. Her bottom still stung a little. She'd not thought he slapped her that hard, yet she had found a blotchy pink outline of a hand on her bottom when she examined herself in the mirror that morning.

'Hey,' Sara said, 'what you think?'

'What do I think of what?'

'We got new captain of detectives. Black woman. Affirmative Action in action.'

Leah nodded noncommittally. She was not about to express an opinion to a chatterbox like Sara Yi about anything controversial, let alone 'Affirmative Action', the Force's attempt to 'encourage' higher levels of minority participation and promotions within its ranks. It had occurred to her on more than one occasion, however, that Affirmative Action was the only reason the flighty young Chinese girl had managed to avoid official sanction on numerous occasions, and even get herself promoted to the detective ranks.

Not that she didn't like Sara Yi. The girl was hard not to like, except for stuffed shirts like Gladwyck, but she acted far too much like an unreliable, fashion conscious, boy crazy teenager for Leah's comfort. She leaned over to whisper, and noticed for the first time the graceful sweep of Sara's throat, startled at how attractive she found it. 'Uhm, you have blue in your hair,' she murmured quietly.

Sara blanched and reached up, her fingers pulling hastily

at her hair. She scrambled in her purse and combed her hair rapidly, muttering in irritation in Mandarin. Or was it Cantonese? 'Cheap hair extensions,' she said apologetically.

'Blue?'

Sara beamed. 'Look real cool. You should try it.'

Leah shook her head.

'I wear last night at rave.'

'You were at a rave on a Monday night?' She imagined the pretty Asian girl dancing and swaying provocatively to pounding music, dressed in something slinky and revealing, and felt a little thrum of heat between her legs that made her blink in astonishment.

'Yeah, very loud, very wild. Didn't get to sleep until four.'

Leah nodded; still stunned to experience sexual interest in another female, let alone Sara. Sometimes she wondered if someone had altered the girl's birth certificate and added three or four, or even five years. She was purported to be twenty-two, but sometimes acted more like seventeen. Not that she wasn't bright and dedicated, but teenagers tended to grate on Leah's need for dignity and circumspection. She might not be a stuffed shirt like Gladwyck, but she had quite high standards for behavior in public. So why on earth would she suddenly find Sara... desirable?

'Nice scarf,' Sara said brightly. 'You buy at Wallmart?'

Leah snorted. 'No, it was a present from a friend. He picked it up in India.' She subconsciously lifted her hand and brushed the soft brown hair back from the side of her face. She was lucky in her hair; it tended to style well and mind its manners. Today it seemed to fairly glow with brightness and life, despite her rough night. It was a deep, sensuous chestnut, a lustrous curtain of rich brown that framed her lovely face immaculately.

Her cheekbones were high and aristocratic, her lips full and seductive, her white teeth giving evidence of a disciplined childhood with the best dentists. Her green eyes were slightly oval, indicating a trace of Mediterranean, or some whispered, Asian ancestry. She was beautiful by anyone's judgment, having the beauty of the predatory cat, not the wispy model. Her eyes could pierce a man to his vitals and she could express more disapproval and contempt with an inclination of her chin than others could with a five-minute verbal diatribe.

She was most certainly not a girl who would allow herself to be spanked. Yet her body seemed to recall each sharp impact of his hand across her raised buttocks, and her ears recalled the sound of flesh spanking flesh as his hand struck, and her mind remembered the sense of outraged excitement as he punished her.

What was wrong with her? She was not a woman given to flights of fancy. Even as a young girl she had not been subject to the swooning romantics of other teenagers. She had always been strong willed, always been smoothly and proudly contained. Her parents had spoiled her with things, but for all intents and purposes she had been alone all her life. That required a certain measure of self-control, and she had come to rely on that self-control in dealings with the world around her, and especially with her cold, aloof parents.

Her father was that dentist who cared for her teeth, an oral surgeon to be specific, while her mother practiced law in Atlanta. As an only (and she thought likely accidental) child, she benefited from her parents' money as well as their desire to have someone else mind her upbringing. She attended boarding schools, and had only to ask for whatever hobby caught her fancy to be enrolled in the appropriate course of instruction.

Thus she moved with the grace instilled by ballet, dance, fencing and martial arts lessons, had quite a talent for both piano and guitar, and was professionally trained in how to apply makeup and style her hair.

Her familiarity with her parents, on the other hand, was somewhat loose. They had seldom played much of a role in her life aside from administering the proper moneys on request and chastising her occasional failures. They had not, needless to say, been pleased with her joining the police. But she had held firm.

Lieutenant Colin Michaels came into the room and took his chair next to Lieutenant Malcolm Phillips.

'I like to jump his bones,' Sara whispered mischievously, her eyes on Michaels.

Leah nodded wordlessly. That was certainly no surprise. Sara had 'jumped the bones' of half the eligible men in the district command. A first generation refugee from Hong Kong who came to the US at nine, she seemed determined to cast off every preconception about Asian women anyone had ever imagined, starting with those relating to how quiet, meek and chaste they were.

Since she was really the only other young female detective in the district her actions did little to persuade the more hidebound males that they were to avoid viewing female police officers as sex objects. This infuriated many of the female officers, quite a few of whom wanted nothing to do with men in any case, and who were outraged at having a 'Chinese boy toy' in their midst.

Leah understood their irritation, but didn't share it. In what she admitted to be a sense of arrogance, she was an island unto herself. She did not believe the actions of a girl like Sara would reflect badly on her, for she was quite obviously a different breed than the giggling girl. But she felt less distant now, given what had happened the other day, and even less given the images now rolling through her thoughts of Sara engaged in lewd carnal acts with Phillips and other men, and then, astonishingly, with her.

'Hello sweets.'

Leah turned, startled out of her shameful reverie, and nodded at Scott Brookline. He'd been her partner when she was promoted to detective a year and a half earlier. There had always been sexual tension between them, for it was quite obvious from the start that he viewed her as an eminently bedable female. Still, he had been professional enough not to try anything beyond a lot of verbal teasing. He was not unattractive, given their ten year age difference, with curly blond hair, a barrel chest and good humored features. But Leah had always been extremely protective of her reputation, and never so much as dated anyone in the police service.

The conversations that filled the room with a hushed babble ceased as a tall, athletic woman entered. It was the new captain, Leah knew at once. She was black, her hair cropped short, nearly to the skull. There was no hint of European or Arabic features in her strong, African face, and something strange deep inside Leah simmered in excitement at a brief thought of herself kneeling at the woman's feet, before she banished it indignantly.

'Good morning,' the woman said, her accent bearing the surprising lilt of one of Britain's fancier private schools. 'I am Captain Taja Mbweni. Prior to assuming this position I was Lieutenant in charge of the robbery squad at Westgate. Prior to that I was a detective sergeant with burglary in Torrance. I have been a police officer for fourteen and a half years.' She stepped around the podium and her eyes moved over the police officers in the room.

She's *hot*, Leah thought, growing aroused despite

herself, inexplicably lurid images rolling through her head.

'I do not expect unquestioned obedience,' Mbweni said, her voice hardening. 'But I expect absolute obedience. If you don't think I am correct you are free to politely and respectfully state the reason for your disagreeing. But anyone caught disobeying my orders in the smallest degree will need to find somewhere else to work. I will not tolerate disobedience anymore than I will tolerate incompetence or laziness.' Her eyes settled on Leah, and she seemed to frown. Then they tightened at the sight of Sara before continuing along their row.

'I am not here to be your friend, your confessor, or your coach. I am here to supervise the detective squads of this district, and you are here to support whatever goals and practices I feel will best serve in policing and maintaining order. I have already met with the senior officers and expressed those policies and goals to them. They will in turn communicate those requirements to you.'

'Jeez, what a bitch,' Sara whispered.

Definitely, Leah silently concurred, but what a hot one! For some bizarre reason she saw her in leather and high heels, glowering down at her from above, and jerked her eyes away, gazing nervously around in fear someone might sense her interest, and wondering where it came from.

'I will meet with each of you privately for a few minutes, however, to help familiarize myself with your strengths and weaknesses. I will express my opinion regarding this to you, and you in turn will consider ways of improving any faults I find in your professional conduct.'

Without a further word she strode straight down the aisle between the silent police officers and out of the door.

'Well, she seems fun,' Scott commented ruefully.

'Too much compensation,' Leah replied. Too many women she knew thought they had to be harder than the men in order to be obeyed and respected, and Mbweni was obviously of that school. But still, she *was* hot.

Lieutenant Patterson silently tacked up a list of detectives' names Captain Mbweni would see, and in what order. It was noted that the female detectives appeared first on the list.

Leah was the fourth, just after Sara. She judged that Mbweni was going to be the punctual type, and arrived only a minute or so before her scheduled time. The door was closed, but she could hear the woman's chilly voice coming from within.

'I don't care about quotas or statistics,' she was saying. 'Your presence is a distraction to the smooth operation of this district station, and the only reason I don't immediately institute a complaint to Internal Affairs to have you fired is that the story would inevitably go public and would make for sensationalist press, which in turn would reflect badly on all of us here. But I will accept your request for transfer by the end of the day. Now get out.'

Leah heard another voice start to speak but Mbweni immediately overrode it. 'I said that will be all,' she snapped, her icy voice rising. 'I find your presence annoying. My advice for you is to resign before you are charged. You are an absolute disgrace to the police service.'

Leah edged back as she sensed movement. The door was yanked open by a black hand and Sara stumbled out, her face ashen, and moved down the corridor in the opposite direction to where Leah stood. Mbweni turned cold eyes on her and jerked her head imperiously.

Leah took a deep breath, then walked into the office and waited anxiously while Mbweni closed the door and went around her desk to sit. The austere woman placed a folder onto a pile of others on her desk, then took one from a second pile, opened and examined it. After a long minute she raised her eyes towards Leah.

'Sit,' she ordered.

Nervous, but doing her best not to show it, Leah sat, her back stiff and her heart pounding a little.

'You have good reviews,' Mbweni said. 'Various reports reflect on your empathy and how this gives you a knack for knowing when people are lying, for knowing what their motivations are. But you have less experience on the street than you should have for a detective, no doubt because you were promoted rapidly, in part due to being female.'

Leah frowned without thinking.

'You think it doesn't play a part?' Mbweni said caustically. 'Don't be naïve. I wouldn't have reached this level this soon had I not been a black lesbian. I am extremely competent but there are many extremely competent white heterosexual males out there who have as much if not more experience than I.' She sat back a little in her chair, her eyes raking Leah.

'You are indeed a fashionable girl,' she said. 'There is nothing in your attire which goes against the letter of the dress code; but you dress too well and too fashionably. You are not here to look attractive, MacInnes. You are not here to impress people with your looks and color-coordinated wardrobe. Tone down your dress. Buy dull grays and blues and blacks, which are looser. A police detective is in plainclothes so as not to be noticed, not to indulge ones taste for stylish fabrics and colours.'

'Yes, ma'am,' Leah said, a little chastened and red-faced.

'You heard what I said to Yi?'

Leah hesitated. 'Yes, ma'am.'

33

'A friend of yours?'

'I like her,' Leah said uncertainly.

'She's a common slut.'

'She does her job well, so far as I've seen,' Leah said loyally.

'Perhaps by the letter of the requirements, but there are unwritten rules at play, MacInnes. A police detective is expected to maintain a professional relationship with his or her colleagues and to be above reproach, even in their private life. Someone who is known to boast about the variety of public places in which she has had sexual intercourse and the wide variety of individuals she has had them with is a fool in too many ways for me to list. Not to mention lacking the dignity needed to uphold the reputation of the service. She has only gotten away with it because she is a visible minority member, and that irritates me immensely, both as a visible minority member and as a female.'

She leaned forward, eyes hard. 'Do you know that I wanted to strike her? I was so utterly outraged with her behavior I wanted to physically thrash her. Given the nature of this service, the old boy network, and the feeling among so many that females can't cut it, I find it appalling to have a female like that in my section. She ought to take up prostitution and put her undoubted talents to work at something she clearly feels a calling for.'

Leah held her breath, feeling again that intense and inexplicable desire to prostrate herself at the woman's feet, a buzzing excitement in the pit of her stomach, and yet at the same time a rising indignation. What a bitch, she thought. 'I... I think you're being a bit harsh, ma'am,' she ventured.

'No doubt the many men here who have sampled her dubious pleasures will agree,' the superior snorted, 'and I

34

expect a lot of protests when the news of her resignation gets out. But it will be interesting to see just who those are who do protest.'

'Why?' Leah asked, frowning. Mbweni's eyes narrowed, but Leah continued. 'It certainly won't be an indication of who has and hasn't slept with her. The cowards won't say boo to you no matter how many times they might have had sex with her. The only ones who will express any reservations are those with, excuse me, the balls to support someone they have some affection for.'

Mbweni smiled coldly. 'Did you use that expression deliberately? Can you imagine how a proud lesbian would view that expression, one which presumes that the bigger one's testicles the braver one is?'

'It's a common expression,' Leah said, 'used metaphorically.' Again she felt that sense of erotic tension, a longing to see Mbweni naked, an almost physical heat at the thought of their bodies pressed together. Yet running counter to it was a rising sense of actual dislike for the woman.

'Yes, used by common people.'

Leah felt her face flushing, and glared across the desk. 'I've never claimed to be up on a pedestal beyond the popular culture of the little people,' she said. 'It has been my experience that placing oneself above others merely sets one up for a very hard and painful fall.'

She was not at all certain why she was daring to argue with a captain. She had certainly never done so before, even the boorish ones like Gladwyck. But something inside her didn't seem to mind if Mbweni was angry with her. Something inside her almost wanted to bait the woman, to anger her so... so she would be punished.

Mbweni smiled thinly. 'Pretty little rich girls always have such confidence.'

'And others have confidence which is of such magnitude it turns to arrogance,' Leah stated. 'And such confidence often turns out to be misplaced.' She felt her stomach clench, wondering if she'd gone too far, her mind still swirling with a potent mixture of arousal, anger, indignation and pride.

'You will tone down your wardrobe,' Mbweni said. 'Pull your hair back and get rid of the flashy jewelry. This isn't a runway or a tea party at the palace. You don't need to light up the eyes of every male you come across.'

'And females?' Leah goaded sarcastically. 'Do you think certain females might find me too attractive to concentrate on their work?'

Mbweni stood up, her eyes cold, and Leah did the same.

'Do you think that merely because you have a pretty face I am attracted to you?' the severe woman demanded.

'Did I suggest that?' Leah asked, putting on a show of casual insolence while her insides knotted with fear.

Mbweni moved around the desk, stopping with her face mere inches from Leah's. Both were tall, but Leah had to tilt her head back fractionally to look into the woman's eyes. She fought to keep still while her heart pounded so strongly she was worried Mbweni would hear it.

'What I would like to do to you, MacInnes,' the fearsome woman hissed, 'is put you across my desk and take a crop to your bottom until you beg to obey my every word.'

Leah's mouth opened in surprise and she felt an almost physical blow of shock in her tummy. Mbweni leaned in even closer until her lips were next to Leah's ear.

'And I don't think that would take very long, MacInnes,' she said in a controlled, threatening tone. 'I think after the first blow you'd be stamping your feet and screaming like a petulant little girl, and after a few more you'd be on

36

your knees with your tongue cleaning my boots.'

'And you'd like that, wouldn't you?' Leah challenged, her voice more defiant than she felt. 'But then you'd be as bad as Sara, letting your pussy get in the way of business. Or is that why you want to get rid of her; because she behaves as she wants to and you wish you could too? Have you had something stiff inside you lately that wasn't made of plastic, captain?'

That *was* too far. Her own behavior shocked her and her stare faltered nervously as she took a half step back.

Mbweni leaned forward, eyes burning, and hissed harshly, 'Get out of my office, MacInnes.'

Chapter Three

The room was still, quiet, and bathed in shadows. Moonlight streaming through the bay window was broken and scattered by small, interlocking diamond-shaped panes. A hesitant moan drifted through the silence, then a drawn out sigh.

To one side of a tall, chrome and mirrored dresser, a large bed squatted partly in the shadows, upon which were a tangle of dark sheets, and beneath them a figure which shifted and turned, twisting without rhythm or reason.

The figure rolled and long, sleep-tousled hair spilled across closed eyes and an open mouth. The head rolled slowly as the body twisted languorously, like a cat stretching. As if drawn by a cord the thin sheets slid slowly downward, revealing ivory skin glowing in the pale light of the moon.

The sheets slid down to reveal full breasts upon a slender ribcage, breasts that rose and fell as the lungs fluttered uncertainly. The sheets continued downward, baring a flat stomach, softly rounded hips, and then the dark 'V' of pubic hair between shapely thighs.

Naked, sighing, Leah twisted onto her side, and then almost immediately slumped back. Her head rolled more slowly and her fingers, resting on the bed beside her, clenched unconsciously.

Slowly, as if drawn by unseen hands, her slender legs shifted apart, spreading fluidly and evenly as the girl continued to sleep. She sighed again and her back arched slightly, pushing firm breasts tautly upward. The pink areolas puckered and swelled, the nipples at their centre stiffening into rigid attention. Leah sighed again, her heels slipping farther apart, knees drawing slowly up, raising her exposed sex.

A shadow slid across the room, darker than night, menacing in its unhurried pace, moving up across the bottom of the bed between Leah's parted legs. It played across her ivory flesh and she gasped, her back arching urgently.

The perfectly smooth flesh of her breasts began to move, to flatten and distend as if squeezed by unseen fingers. It flowed and shifted, the nipples turning and twisting. Leah's breathing became quicker, more ragged, and she whimpered in her sleep.

The tight lips of her sex seemed to quiver, and then gently ease apart to reveal her glistening vagina. Her clitoris swelled wetly, quivering like an eager antenna in search of stimulus. Then the inner lips were gently pushed in and back, her inner tunnel opening and blossoming wide. Her breathing became deeper, a flush spreading over her body. The flesh of her breasts seemed to ripple unceasingly, her erect nipples rolling from side to side.

She groaned aloud, her back arching fully as she took her weight on her shoulders, her fingers clawing the sheets at her sides. She fell back to the mattress, only to arch again, and then again.

The lips of her sex pushed out, and then drew back within her body, repeating continually as she began to gasp rhythmically in her troubled sleep. Her body lurched and the bed began to creak gently in time to her movements.

She fled across the plain, light shift flying about her as she ran pell-mell through the tall grass. Behind her were the screams and shrieks of the other girls and the coarse yells and cries of victory from the raiders. Then, rising above it, the terrifying sound of a horse's hooves pounding against the earth, and growing closer.

She risked a look back, and cried out in horror to see the horse bearing down on her. She turned and twisted, trying to dodge, searching for any cover that might protect her. Exhausted she ran faster, desperate in her hopeless race.

She screamed as a hand yanked on her hair, the horse up beside her now, slowing, its rider yanking back viciously on its reins. Her hands jerked back behind her, seizing the stout wrist of the hand embedded in her tangled hair. 'No!' she screamed.

Mocking laughter replied, and she screamed again as she was drawn up as if weightless, lifted and draped across the shoulders of the powerful horse. A harsh slap across her buttocks made her cry out again as a harsh voice said something in a language she did not recognize.

The horse turned and trotted back, Leah bouncing helplessly, a powerful hand on her neck pinning her down as another roughly pawed her bottom through the thin shift and between her slender thighs.

Her wrists were seized, pulled up together and crossed behind her back, then a rough leather thong was twisted around them to pin them there as the horse returned to the edge of the small village. The cries and moans of pain and fear rose around her as the horse trotted through them, and Leah strained to raise her head, trying to peer through her tangled hair at the fiery remnants of the village, and the bodies littering the streets.

The horse stopped, snorting heavily. There was a harsh

grunt of male voices and her hair was cruelly yanked up, causing her to scream, sliding, and then falling back off the horse to be caught by another man. He laughed and filled his hands with her breasts, squeezing painfully.

Another man, hairy and leering, gripping the front of her shift and tore it open and off. Leah screamed in terror, filled with shame and horror as she was flung down on the steps of the church, legs spread wide. The first man knelt between them, and when she tried to twist away he impatiently slapped her with the back of a huge hand, sending her head reeling to one side, blood filling her mouth. He sniggered in drunken delight and tore his cock free of his greasy breeches, then pressed it against her naked sex and thrust deep into her body.

It should have hurt her, yet there was no pain, only the deep, soft, lush feel of her pussy spreading wide and wetly enveloping the thick cock, and pleasure rushed through her. The man's cock drove deep and then she did feel some discomfort, but it was almost nothing alongside the wondrous sense of delight at being so fully penetrated, so filled with him. Gasping, wide-eyed but horrified, she stared up at her leering assailant, at the half-dozen men standing around them on the steps, goading the grunting man on, awaiting their turn.

The cock retreated, then penetrated deep again, another wonderful rush of pleasure permeating her body and soul. The man lowered his face and gnawed her nipples, growling bites that shouldn't have made her breasts quiver with delight – but did.

His coarse hands dug into the soft flesh of her backside, jerking her up to meet his bull-like thrusting, and Leah gasped and moaned and whimpered as she was cruelly used, ravished before the leering men gathered around. Dazed, bewildered, she stared up at them, shamed and lost and wondering.

The climax rolled through her with unstoppable power, and she shuddered uncontrollably against him. Her face burned with disgrace as the watchers cackled and pointed; yet she could not control her body's responses. Her head rolled from side to side as she arched her back repeatedly, gasping in unison with the steady, aggressive thrusting of the rigid cock inside her.

The orgasm rolled on and on, and it was glorious. She dared not breath for fear it would help to dissipate the incredible pleasure sweeping through her. But it relented finally, only to leave her gripped by a terrible need for more.

The man groaned and hurried his pace; his hips hammering down like a piston against her softness. He shuddered and dipped his back, coming inside her, spewing his male seed within her belly. He grunted and slumped away, and Leah laying exhausted and panting as another took his place.

Again she began to moan in time to eager, animalistic thrusts. Again her senses spiraled upward into ecstasy, shuddering as an even more powerful orgasm rocked her.

On and on it went, men shuffling away from the steps drained and satisfied, others arriving to join the lurid onlookers, to wait their turn between her legs. One, less patient, knelt on the top step next to her head and seized her hair, positioning her face as he wanted and sinking his erection into her gasping mouth.

Through her delirium Leah tasted sweat and grime and urine, and gloried in it. Alien tastes that filled her mouth, the bloated cock pressing her tongue down, stretching her cheeks outward and buffeting the roof of her mouth. She sucked as best she could as it began to pump in and out between her stretched lips, her tongue flitting eagerly against the underside of the head.

Her hair was twisted and pulled, her neck aching, yet none of that mattered. She sucked and licked hungrily at the hard male organ, suckling desperately as it exploded within her mouth, filling her with warm, salty liquid.

All afternoon they fucked her, one and two at a time. As the sun set she knelt in the porch of the church, her face and breasts coated with drying semen, her cheek pressed against the aged wood floorboards, her wrists still bound behind her back, her bottom raised as yet another man fucked her fiercely from behind. She was utterly exhausted, drained to the edge of unconsciousness by the continuous physical abuse, rough handling, and emotional overload.

And then she was on her feet, staggering, dragged to face one of the wooden stakes erected in the village square. Her wrists were untied then rebound before her, raised above her and secured to a heavy iron ring set in the stake.

The soft flesh of her breasts pushed uncomfortably against the roughly cut wood, and she slumped there, exhausted, her head lolling back. Despite the pain in her aching body she was still gripped with sexual excitement, tempting her to squeeze her thighs together around the sturdy, uneven post.

A crack of noise and pain made her scream, throwing her harshly against the creaking wooden support. Her head twisted around and she stared back at the leering man holding the long length of leather, stared in dazed incomprehension as he drew his arm back and then flung it forward again. Her eyes flinched away, her head turning, and then she felt it slash across her shoulders. She screamed and jerked as mocking jeers rose around her.

Another lash across her shoulders… another across her

lower back… another across her bottom. Fire laced her pale flesh and spilled tears from her eyes. Yet her inner fires remained hot, some dark side of her mind exulting in being the focus of such shocking and outrageous cruelty.

Welt after welt rose on her back, ugly red lines of fiery pain marring the soft white canvas of flesh. The pain rose, and yet so too did the heat and dark pleasure. She slouched by her wrists, yet did so in a way that subconsciously or not offered her bottom out towards the bite of the whip. Fire and pain slashed across it again and again and again, and a terrible temptation rose within her to open her thighs.

And then the man was beside her, tugging on her hair, leering down at her. He held the whip, a long, dangerous, ugly looking thing attached to a scarred handle, which he reversed in his hand as she stared at it through glassy eyes. He lowered the handle out of her sight and she felt it probing between her buttocks, and then…

Leah cried out as he penetrated her, as he pressed the braided leather handle into her recently violated sex, as he pushed it deep and began to pump it in and out. The dark pleasure swirled around her as males laughed, and she felt the climax exploding within her with a force she could barely believe.

And then the raiders moved on, wagons heavily laden with plunder, horsemen swaying drunkenly from their saddles. With her arms stretched out before her, wrists bound with leather thongs, Leah trotted dazedly after them, roped to the saddle of one of her captors, naked as she had been all afternoon, panting wearily, her bare feet shuffling through the wet earth of the road on her journey to slavery.

44

Sun filled the room with light, and Leah moaned and jerked awake, staring wildly around her. A dream, she thought weakly, just a dream. And yet, perhaps it was more.

Though it was chilly in the room the covers were thrown back, and she gasped as her fingers crept between her thighs and lifted away wet and glistening. She stared at them, then down at herself. Her body was coated in slippery fluids, most especially between her thighs. She felt raw aching inside, and her thighs, bottom and breasts felt bruised and tender.

With a cry of revulsion she leapt from the bed and stared down at her body, aghast at the slick, slimy liquid almost covering her face and breasts and stomach, and seeping slowly down her thighs from her sopping pussy.

She hurried into the bathroom, snatching at paper towels at first, trying to rub off the nauseating unguent. She got into the shower, turning it on as hot as she could bear, and winced as her fingers moved tentatively down between her legs, feeling the swollen lips of her sex, trembling as they moved anxiously against them.

How and what were the words that spun through her dazed, confused mind as she soaped herself repeatedly.

And the dream did not fade, as dreams normally did. It was clear and vivid in her mind, like a recent memory. She shuddered as she clutched her arms around her soapy breasts, remembering and almost feeling the harsh fingers digging into them, feeling the broken-toothed mouths chewing and sucking and slobbering. She could still feel their calloused hands mauling her body, still remember the feel of their cocks thrusting into her.

Yet as she stepped out of the shower, her body cleansed and rosy pink, she saw no sign of bruising or welts. Her breasts felt tender, but there was no focus to the pain. Her back felt sore, but looking over her shoulder in the mirror showed it was still smooth and unmarked, although she shuddered at the clear memory of the lashes laid across her poor flesh.

But of course it was only a dream. It had never really happened. It had been a strange and twisted dream…

But then Leah froze, unable to understand the slime that had covered her face and hair and body, which she had tasted on her tongue and in the back of her throat, and knew to be semen.

She put on the most diaphanous of silk shifts, one that barely descended below her buttocks, but it was sufficient covering for now. She wrapped her hair in a towel and left the bathroom, suddenly having a desperate need for some caffeine.

With a cup of strong black coffee inside her she felt a little better and returned to the bathroom, removed the towel and dried her hair, letting the hot, comforting air blow through her silken tresses, her thoughts still preoccupied by the bizarre dream. Had it some relation to Morales? She had never really gone for the darker side of sexuality before, or hadn't thought she had. Yet he'd coerced her into his perverse clutches so quickly and with such contemptuous ease, and despite her normally rigid professional and personal standards she had allowed it to happen… and found it shockingly exciting.

Had the experience awoken some dark side of her nature that hungered for danger… and dangerous men? No, the very thought angered and unsettled her. She had always considered herself a strong, independently minded woman. She was surely not a submissive girl who craved to kneel before a dominant being and beg their favor.

And yet in sexual terms she found the notion of doing so deeply erotic. And hadn't the bizarre and unexpected thought of prostrating herself in front of Mbweni made her almost breathless with illicit excitement?

It was warm in the bathroom as she set the dryer down, yet the outline of her stiff nipples was clear against the thin silk of her shift. She licked her lips a trifle nervously and tentatively cupped her breasts, feeling the tender buds pressing into the palms of her hands. She was not aroused. No, she was not!

'What do you say, girl?'

Leah made a face and sat back on the edge of the desk. 'Odd, I'll grant you.'

Scott raised his eyebrows from the monitor. It was showing the tape from the building's security camera, from very early that morning. Samantha Partridge was on the tape, walking out of her parents' pricey apartment, along the hall to the elevator, down into the lobby, and then out the front door. She walked slowly and calmly, with no apparent concern on her face. Nor, apparently, any worry at being seen. Well, it was the early morning hours. Then again, she was entirely nude.

'Looks almost like she's sleepwalking,' he said.

'It does kind of, doesn't it?' Leah agreed.

'By all accounts she had no worries, no stress.'

'And according to her sister she never ever slept in the nude,' Leah said.

'Still, there's nothing else to conclude from the tape,' Scott decided. 'Nobody forced her to go out like that.'

'But where is she? Surely a nude girl walking the streets would be noticed and helped or reported, even in the early hours. Someone would have seen and called us.'

'Unless the first person to see her snatched her,' Scott suggested.

'That would be really bad luck,' Leah said, somewhat

47

sarcastically, 'falling into the clutches of a passing abductor when sleepwalking.'

'Maybe she was in the road and got hit by a car, and now she's in a hospital somewhere.'

Leah shook her head. 'No, we've checked.'

Scott looked out the window frustratedly. 'So how's this for an idea,' he said after a few minutes, 'she was hypnotized.'

'Hypnotized?' Leah echoed, unconvinced.

'Just a thought,' he said, without much conviction. 'Suppose she was seeing one of those hypnotists who claim to help with bad habits and phobias and he or she planted a suggestion for her to leave home.'

'Come on,' Leah scoffed.

'You know those other girls disappeared from their beds at night, too,' Scott went on, clutching at straws. 'No one saw them go, but there's no evidence they took any clothing with them. Their nightgowns were left discarded on the bed or floor. We've always assumed they put some clothes on before disappearing, but suppose they didn't? Suppose they were nude when they left home, too?'

'You make that suggestion to Lieutenant Michaels and he'll hand you your head,' Leah warned. 'It's pure speculation – and not very good speculation, at that. We don't even know if this girl's disappearance is related to the others.'

Scott looked up at her. 'Now who's kidding who?' he snorted. 'She's a dead-ringer for both the Anderson girl and the Phillips girl. The three of them could be sisters.'

Leah sighed and nodded her agreement. It was the strangest part of the disappearances. That Anderson and Phillips looked so remarkably alike had raised a lot of eyebrows given that, so far as they knew, they'd never met and had no points of contact. That someone had

48

managed to find such two similar girls in the city was little short of amazing. That he'd found three, if that were the case, bordered on the impossible. From their enquiries they knew the girls were the same height, the same weight, and they had almost exactly the same measurements. They were blue-eyed and blonde, their hair styled virtually the same, and their attractive features were very similar, too. They could almost be twins – or triplets, now.

They took the tape and walked out through the marble foyer. Their car was parked by the entrance steps, and Leah drew her trench coat around her as she stepped down to it and the cool wind whistled through the canyon made by the tall buildings.

'It was cold last night,' Scott said as he unlocked the car and got in.

'You'd think that would have woken her,' Leah said, getting in beside him and closing her door. 'We'll have to check with someone who knows about sleepwalking.'

'How about Gladwyck?' Scott chuckled. 'He sleepwalks through his job every day.' He started the car and pulled out into the street.

'I'm actually coming to appreciate superiors who sit in their office all day and don't bother me,' she said.

He snorted. 'That new captain is something else again, ain't she?'

Leah nodded. 'She's getting on my nerves,' she admitted. But more than that she was making her nervous. Too many times she'd felt a chill at the back of her neck, turned, and seen Mbweni looking at her. And whenever she did the woman would kind of smirk knowingly, look her up and down, then turn away.

Leah thought of the things she said, and a little rush of heat swept down through her belly into her panties. The thought of being bound naked before the woman made her chest tight. Her nipples hardened at once, transmitting little quivers of pleasure through her breasts as she moved, as they moved within the tight confines of her bra cups. The fact that she disliked the arrogant woman made little difference to her physical reactions.

'Well, maybe a little discipline is what the district needs,' Scott suggested without conviction. 'It seems to have done wonders for Yi.'

Leah frowned uncertainly. Sara had certainly become far more tightlipped since her meeting with Mbweni. She wasn't her usual bouncy self, and her eyes looked haunted. Since there had been no announcement and she'd not wanted to embarrass the girl by telling her she'd overheard the transfer ultimatum, she hadn't really been able to discuss it with her. The few times she had tried to offer a chance for Sara to talk to her the girl had abruptly shirked away. Leah shrugged dismissively, looking out the window at the passing traffic. She had her own problems, after all, and Mbweni was the least of them.

It had been almost a week now since she had interviewed Morales. During the day her mind was filled with erotic flights of fancy involving herself and almost everyone she knew. It was bizarre. She kept fantasizing about people, both men and women, about police colleagues she'd known for years, people who lived in her building, witnesses she'd spoken to, schoolgirls she passed on the street, and even that bitch Mbweni, for that matter. And Sara, and Scott. And they weren't idle thoughts either, but brooding fantasies that made her breasts rise and fall more rapidly as her breathing quickened, made her abdominal muscles clench and her pussy warm and moisten.

It had been bad enough that first day, but it was getting worse as time went by. She walked through the day in a cloud of sexual hunger, often finding it difficult to concentrate on her job as erotic fantasies spilled through her mind. Even watching the girl on the tape had made her nipples ache as she'd imagined having sex with her, then with Scott while they watched, then with both of them together.

And the nights were worse. She was masturbating every evening now, and then more after she climbed into bed to toss and turn throughout the night, her dreams filled with shameful submission to men and women. That first melancholic nightmare had been played out again and again in different settings in her sleeping mind. Every night in her dreams she was fucked roughly, climaxing again and again, and every morning she woke feeling as though she'd been the centerpiece of a gangbang.

She had twice given herself to strangers she'd met while desperately prowling nightclubs. The sex was desperate and carnal, and she climaxed repeatedly. But it was short-lived, as well, and left her feeling ashamed and dirty as she made her way home, although her body had a terrible craving she could not satisfy.

'Doing anything much this weekend?'

She blinked in surprise and turned to Scott. 'Um, no, I don't think so.'

That night she could barely get through the door to her apartment before tearing off her clothes. She felt free, alive, as she padded back and forth, naked, her hands running up and down her body, cupping her breasts, fingering her swollen nipples, moving down to her hips and round to her buttocks.

Her apartment, number R3, was small and oddly shaped. It was a leftover, a kind of architectural surplus in the design of the building. It was on the top floor, which she shared with the various utility maintenance rooms, but the building owners had decided to maximize their income and create an odd little apartment. But at least compared to the rest of the building it was quite cheap, and after selling a small house her aunt had left her Leah was able to purchase it, with the help of a mortgage.

In the day the apartment was filled with light, and at night she drew the blue, vertical blinds and let her small lamps, and the reflected light from her aquarium fill it with soft, comforting blue-green light.

Leah paced back and forth. All the blinds were open, but she had few fears of voyeurs. The only light in the apartment came from the gas fireplace, the flames dancing around ornate stone 'logs', the watery light from her aquarium, and the glow of the moon through the windows, washing her flesh in pale white as she moved back and forth, filled with nervous energy and the sexual hunger that never seemed to go away.

The burr of her phone startled her. She stared at it for a few moments, and then picked it up. 'Hello?'

'Detective MacInnes?' The voice was a deep purr, the tone somehow both mocking and threatening.

'Yes.'

'This is Captain Mbweni.'

She knew it, but she was startled regardless. 'Yes?' she said again, wondering what Mbweni would think or say if she knew she was naked at that moment. She felt a low buzz of arousal between her thighs as she stroked a hand up her bare belly.

'I have been looking over the progress, or lack of progress, of the recent case involving the missing girls. I am not happy.'

And why, Leah wondered, would a captain bother to express her unhappiness to a lowly detective? But she said nothing.

'I have decided that rearranging some of the detective pairings will allow for a new outlook on this case, so I have placed you with Yi for the time being.'

Leah, standing before her window and looking out at the city, blinked in astonishment. 'But I thought—'

'I'm sure you'll be an excellent influence on her,' Mbweni went on, 'calm her down, help me to instill some discipline in her.'

'I guess,' Leah said warily. 'But I thought she was, um, transferring.'

'Whatever gave you that idea?' Mbweni's voice fairly purred.

'Well, the other day—'

'Eavesdropping is not something you want to be bragging about, young lady, now is it?'

'I wasn't—'

'Not that curiosity isn't a necessary feature in a good officer, of course.'

'It was my impression, ma'am,' Leah said in a tone bordering on insolent, 'that you so disapprove of Sara's off duty behavior you wish her gone.'

'Any woman with morals would disapprove of cheap behavior, MacInnes,' Mbweni said, her voice icy. 'But if a situation presents itself which might be to one's advantage, then one can make use of such a person.'

'I... I don't understand, ma'am,' Leah admitted.

'No, of course you don't.' The woman sighed impatiently down the phone. 'Do you not think the motivation for the disappearance of three attractive girls has a sexual component, officer?'

'Almost certainly,' Leah agreed, 'yes.'

'Then perhaps a creature as sexually active and loose as Yi might give us some insight, however unintentional,

53

'into that mindset.'

'I don't see what you're getting at,' Leah said.

'Don't be so naïve, MacInnes,' Mbweni said dismissively. 'It's instinctive. You do it yourself.'

'Excuse me?' Leah said angrily. 'I'm not altogether sure what you mean by that, but it sounds highly offensive and it's thoroughly unprofessional of you to make such a comment.'

'Who decides what constitutes professionalism, MacInnes?' Mbweni growled. 'A lowly detective or the captain she works for?'

'I'm sure a board of professional standards would make a neutral party,' Leah snapped, but she heard Mbweni laugh mockingly.

'I know the ins and outs of professional standards better than you can ever imagine, young lady,' the woman warned. 'If you try to involve yourself in it I will twist you around like a pretzel and make you look as incompetent, mindless and pathetic as that disgraceful slut Yi. You do not want me for an enemy; believe me. And especially when I could be so helpful to you.'

'Helpful?' Leah asked guardedly.

'As I said earlier, there are any number of ways I can take advantage of a girl like Yi; assignments I would not dare use most female officers for. She could infiltrate prostitution rings or strip clubs, for example, where the perpetrators of these disappearances may frequent.'

Leah stared openmouthed out of the window. 'Are… are you suggesting…?'

'I hardly think a girl who so enjoys flaunting her body would be traumatized by stripping before an audience,' Mbweni confirmed. 'And as morally loose as Yi is, asking her to sleep with a suspect should hardly produce too much coyness.'

'That's outrageous!' Leah exclaimed, although for some inexplicable reason the thought of going to such lengths to work undercover secretly made her pulse quicken.

'Oh, come now,' Mbweni said persuasively, 'less of the shocked little Miss Innocent. It's not like I've asked you to do it. Not that you wouldn't make a lovely stripper, of course, dancing before a room filled with horny men... and perhaps a horny woman or two...'

Leah felt her breath leave her at the words, at the undertones behind them, at the way their minds were working so closely. 'A horny woman like... like you, perhaps?' Leah ventured, though she didn't know why she felt so compelled to ask.

There was a pause. 'I wouldn't turn my head away,' Mbweni said, her voice silky. 'No, I certainly wouldn't.'

Another shock hit Leah's belly, and she slid a hand down between her legs, rubbing a finger lightly against her swelling clitoris. 'Well I'm sorry to have to disappoint you,' Leah said, her voice tense.

'You haven't disappointed me... yet,' Mbweni purred. 'But remember how *helpful* a captain can be to your career, officer. An intelligent young woman like you could be on the promotional ladder in no time at all. But on the other hand, well, it would be such a pity to see your career hindered by all those sexist males who see you as nothing more than breeding material.'

'Unlike you,' Leah said, shifting her feet apart and leaning her back against the wall as she curled a finger and slid it into the tightness of her sex. Despite an intense sense of shame and confusion at her actions, she felt a hot flush of excitement and daring, knowing Mbweni would have no idea what she was doing.

'Yi is a cheap, weak-willed tart, MacInnes,' Mbweni went on. 'I could have her on her knees between my legs in an instant if I wanted her. Perhaps I even will, just to amuse myself. But you're a stronger type of female altogether, though not an equal to me, of course.'

'What exactly are you proposing?' Leah demanded, trying to keep her tone belligerent to signal her opposition to the woman's plans.

'Let us just see if we can reach an accommodation which will be mutually beneficial,' the woman said, her tone now appeasing.

Leah faltered. Despite her dislike of the woman it was undeniably true that if Mbweni wanted to help her career she almost certainly could. It was equally true that most of the senior detectives she encountered were discriminatory bigots who thought of her as a dumb broad who had been taken in due to gender equality provisions.

But all this practicality aside, she was also fighting against the realization that the thought of being submissive in Mbweni's presence was making her breathless, making her legs unsteady, which was why she needed the support of the wall. Her pride and dislike of the woman made the thoughts spinning around her head extremely difficult to accept, but she now had two fingers inside her and was fighting to keep her voice steady. 'And would this mutual accommodation involve… after work activities?' she asked tightly.

'A young detective who becomes the aid of a senior office is at his or her beck and call at all hours of the day and night, officer,' came the answer down the phone, the voice without apparent emotion. 'Surely you're aware of that.'

Leah had to fight this. She could not give in, she could not bow and scrape before the arrogant bitch. And what if Mbweni was merely pretending to be interested? What if she merely wanted Leah to acquiesce so she had a hold over her? 'I… I'm not going to trade my soul for a promotion,' Leah said weakly, 'nor my body.'

Mbweni chuckled throatily. 'Why, my dear, I wouldn't want you if you did. That would make you almost as weak as Yi. After all, a lovely young lady like you could probably engineer endless opportunities with senior male officers to get the same thing, and I wouldn't want someone who would willingly trade herself for promotion.'

Leah was bemused, finding it hard to think straight, feeling she was being easily toyed with. 'Then, what…?'

'The accommodation I have in mind, MacInnes, is not one between equals,' the disembodied voice told her. 'It is when the weak acknowledges the strength of her superior, abandons the pretense of independence, and does as she is told.'

'That doesn't sound like something I'm interested in,' Leah said, the shadow of her hand still moving rhythmically between her thighs, and she slid down the wall to her haunches, dreamily inserting a third finger into her wet pussy as she talked.

'I know, my dear. That's what makes it all the more interesting.'

The phone went dead and Leah put the receiver back in its cradle, shaking her head.

She ran her free hand slowly up her side, cupping her breasts and flicking her thumb across one erect nipple. Unwelcome but darkly arousing images of her and Mbweni naked came to her mind, of herself on her knees before the tall woman, and despite disliking her the images provoked a hot thrill within her body and her breath to falter in her lungs.

A bitch, that's what the woman was. But she was a strong and powerful bitch, and very attractive. A week

57

ago she would have cringed at the thought of sleeping with another woman, but since meeting her new superior officer she had begun to fantasize about it more and more. It was inexplicable and shameful for someone with such staunch moral parameters to even consider such a thing… but it was also breathlessly enticing.

Being 'conquered' by Mbweni might just be extraordinarily exciting…

But damn it, she was not that bitch's plaything! She was a strong and determined professional woman, and she would not be toyed with by anybody!

She slid back up the wall to her feet, pulling her moist fingers from her sex, and moved towards the bedroom. She paused, staring out the window, then pulled open the door to the balcony and stepped outside.

Twenty floors up the chill wind swirled around her, lifting her hair and raising goose bumps on her skin. She moved to the rail, a stainless steel tube frame with clear glass beneath, and leaned over, staring down at the car park and the entrance to the building. Her outer body felt the chill, but the heat within her only grew more intense. It was being naked out of doors, as she was, open to anybody's eyes.

There were a few nearby buildings with lights lit up and down their darkened sides. No doubt there were other people out on their balconies, a few, at least, but she could pick out none in the darkness. She bent from the waist, letting her breasts press against the cold steel of the rail, feeling the chill run through her nipples, and in doing so her bottom was pushed out and her feet almost subconsciously slid aside on the floor, as though she was positioning herself in readiness to be fucked from behind by a secret lover.

It was how Morales had fucked her as she knelt shackled

to the posts. She had her arms stretched along the top of the cylindrical steel rail, shuddering a little as she shifted her feet farther apart, raising her bottom and easing it back a little more, letting her breasts sway, cool as the breeze wafted around them yet tingling with her excitement.

How would Mbweni take advantage of her, she wondered? Would she force her to her knees and instruct her how to please her with her mouth? She imagined she could feel the woman's strong fingers in her hair, guiding her face towards her sex, and felt her pussy spasming and her body thrumming with sexual yearning.

A shadow moved over her, a cloud passing across the moon. She looked up, and the hair rose on her neck. Nothing was there. Nothing. Yet she felt a presence that both aroused and terrified her. She sensed movement behind her, yet did nothing, her heart pounding, her pulse racing, fear clutching her body. She felt an icy finger against her spine, between her shoulders. She gasped with shock, yet could not straighten up or turn her head. She felt as though she were in a dream, desperate to run yet unable to move, desperate to turn and defend herself, desperate to make her body comply with her instincts.

The finger slid slowly down her spine, leaving a trail of icy fire behind, between her buttocks, and then prodded lightly at her tightly closed anus. Then the finger was joined by others, becoming a hand squeezing her bottom, a cold hand that possessively kneaded her trembling flesh.

A length of black silk a couple of inches wide dropped onto one of her wrists, and her head turned ever so slowly to stare as the whispering material seemed to move on its own, a long length of oily black wrapping around and around her wrist, layer after layer falling across her arm, moving upwards to her elbow, then past it to her upper

59

arm, circling tightly, binding her warm flesh firmly to the cold steel of the rail. It continued across her shoulder, slithering snakelike, then began to wind its way down around her other arm as the hand continued to caress her bottom, and then the backs of her thighs. Whimpering, she felt another hand slip over her hip, a chilly finger laying against her sex and then rubbing ever so softly. She jerked, gasping, and then moaned as the finger curled and pierced her body.

She felt something at her feet, something which could only be the same soft silk, sliding slowly around both ankles then tugging insistently, forcing her feet farther apart.

She yelped at a stinging blow to her bottom, gasping and staring into the night. Fingers began to knead her breasts, twisting, rolling and stroking her nipples, then pinching cruelly so that she winced with each needle of pain.

The finger was ice-cold inside her, but she felt herself growing helplessly moist around it, felt her juices flowing, down her thighs as the finger pushed deeper... impossibly deep. Another crack of pain made her bottom quiver and she thought she heard, almost inaudible, a throaty chuckle.

The finger drew back, and then something larger, thicker, more rigid, prodded against her wet opening. As icy as the finger it pushed in slowly at first, and then thrust sharply. And with the pain the hard thrust induced a climax that set her body convulsing. Another thrust drove deep, and drew a cry of pain and feverish pleasure from her lips.

Machine-like the stalk began to stroke into her body, moving ever faster, driving to the deepest depths of her without the feel of a body ever touching her bottom. It filled her with cold, but Leah felt another shattering orgasm sweep through her. She cried out again, twisting violently, feeling the tightness of the silk strips binding her arms to the rail and holding her ankles wide.

A crack of pain across her buttocks made her cry out, and again she heard – almost heard – a throaty chuckle. Her eyes were wide as they stared down at the car park below, her mouth open as her breaths came in deep, ragged gulps, and she orgasmed.

But still her body was jolted forward again and again by the deep thrusts of the cold rigidity within, and her hair spilled over her face as she wailed in wondering pleasure and discomfort. Her mind, overwhelmed by the intensity of raw need and hunger, tumbled amid the waves of bliss as her body was used violently by a force she did not understand.

She felt another numbing crack across her raised bottom. Her breasts were squeezed and kneaded by harsh hands, her nipples tugged, and then she sensed a hovering presence just behind her head. Her hair was tugged back and she felt a sudden sharp stab at the nape of her neck. She screamed in agony, yet the agony was washed away almost at once. A crescendo of pleasure that made everything else pale into insignificance tore through her nervous system, and her voice rose in a long, undulating scream of ecstasy.

She collapsed against the rail, limp, chest heaving. Dazedly she heard doors sliding open in the apartments below, people stepping out onto balconies, muttering unintelligible comments. The silk strips unwound and she sagged to the floor of her balcony, slumping onto her back, panting for breath as she stared up into the moon.

Chapter Four

Leah rolled over with a sleepy groan, her eyes fluttering for a moment. She brought her hands up and rubbed the sleep from her eyes, then yawned. It felt as if she'd only just gotten to sleep.

Grumpily she slapped the alarm and stilled its buzzing. She lay on her back, naked but for the sheets bunched across her midriff. She did not normally sleep naked but her skin felt tender to the touch when she went to bed, and she'd not wanted to feel anything against it. She'd even replaced her normal cotton sheets with the black satin set she bought on a silly romantic whim a week into her last relationship.

Her skin still felt raw, but there was nothing to see but healthy pink flesh. She sat up, her eyes dropping to her breasts. When she went to bed they'd felt bruised and sore, but that had faded and there were no marks to see. Her hand dropped lightly to her groin and she winced ever so slightly. She was still tender there.

Her mind shied away from thinking about what had happened to her. It was Friday, and she had work to go to.

It was a struggle to lift herself out of bed, but she did and shuffled her way to the kitchen, turned on the coffee, then shuffled to the bathroom. Having showered she felt a little better, until she caught something out of the corner of her eye, half turned and looked closer, and then her stomach fell at the very visible image of a blotchy handprint across her bare buttocks. Her pulse quickened and she grasped the edge of the basin to keep her legs from buckling at the incomprehensible and disturbing discovery. She remembered with shocking clarity the pain, as if... as if someone had spanked her.

She tore her eyes away, struggling to deny what she saw, stumbling out the door and hurrying to the kitchen for a mug of hot, strong coffee.

'Good morning, detective.'

'Good morning, sergeant,' Leah returned, as she pushed through the office door. She wore a sleeveless black turtleneck sweater beneath a cream linen suit jacket. The sweater was a little too formfitting for work, but the jacket offset it, and more importantly it hid the bruising on the nape of her neck.

She continued on to the briefing room, where she found her colleagues gathered around the long tables, and Sara sitting amongst them, uncharacteristically quiet, her back rigid. Her dark hair was tied in a pair of loose pigtails, which gave her an oddly young and out of place look for a police detective, and she wore a dark blue blazer. Leah sat next to her, smiling, but Sara did not smile back.

'Mbweni's been playing God again,' Leah whispered, and Sara nodded. 'Is something wrong?'

'Nothing,' the girl said, not looking at Leah.

Lieutenant Trask stood and moved behind the podium, and the muttered conversations went still.

'As you all know, we've had a small break in the case,' he started. 'The startling similarity between the missing girls and the fact that none of them knew the other means our fellow must have some kind of access to a picture database, and that's offered up a whole new area for us to investigate.' He rubbed his hands and smiled grimly.

'We'll be looking into school and college databases first to see which ones contain pictures. Right now we know that many of them do. We'll also be looking into such things as photography firms and organizations that develop film. We'll also be checking the Internet. But we don't know for a fact that our fellow only accesses one database. He could be trawling multiple systems, so we'll want to check into the feasibility of that as well.'

He leaned forward against the podium and scowled out at them.

'There is more than sufficient information out there, more than enough evidence for us to determine who this fellow is,' he said sternly. 'You simply haven't put it together yet.'

'It went from *we* to *us* pretty quick,' Leah muttered to Sara.

'None of these girls have turned up anywhere yet,' Trask continued, 'and we believe they're still being held. I want everyone to put in their best effort at solving these disappearances.'

'As opposed to doing nothing, I suppose,' Leah mumbled resentfully, so only she and Sara could hear.

They were assigned to visit a group of Internet service providers to find out how easy it would be for outside people to get such records from schools and colleges. Everyone rose more or less at the same time, and it was only then that Leah noticed Sara was wearing a daringly short tartan skirt with her blazer, really showing off her slender legs.

'Let's go,' the girl said brusquely, snatching up her purse and marching off before Leah could ask why she was wearing such a revealing skirt when on duty, but Leah noticed male heads turning in her wake as lecherous eyes followed her exit.

Leah hurried to catch her up, and from behind, with her pigtails, blazer, and tartan pleated skirt, it looked very much like she was chasing a schoolgirl, although she suspected any school principle would send a girl home for wearing a skirt that short, and she could only wonder what Mbweni would think of it. It was probably, she thought, a silent show of rebellion against Mbweni, and she doubted it would be tolerated for long. She caught up with the petit girl, but Sara's eyes remained fixed straight ahead as they reached the stairs and took them down to the car park.

'I'll drive,' Leah said, and Sara didn't reply. They got into the car and Leah turned to Sara, the tartan skirt high around her thighs and giving a glimpse of white silk panties.

'Okay, what's with the skirt?' she asked.

'There's nothing wrong with my skirt,' Sara replied, scowling.

'It's way too short,' Leah argued. 'And why the pigtails? Are you going undercover in a school or something?'

'I not tell you how to do your hair, you not tell me how to do mine,' the Asian girl snapped.

'But you're hardly looking very professional, that's all I'm saying.'

'So?' Sara snapped uncompromisingly. 'Why do that matter?'

'It matters if you want people to treat you seriously as a police officer,' Leah said in exasperation.

'I not worried what people think,' the girl stubbornly insisted.

Leah shook her head, turned the ignition and headed for the street, but found her eyes flitting repeatedly to the sight of the Asian girl's naked thighs and cheeky peep of her panties. They were lovely legs and she found, despite her irritation at doing so, that she began to dwell on what lay beneath the soft silk, and then to the rest of the girl's body. What would Sara be like in bed, she wondered? Wild, she thought, and uninhibited. Had she any experience with women? Knowing Sara, quite possibly.

Leah's eyes continued to glance sideways and secretly admire the lithe form of the girl beside her whenever the road ahead was clear for a few seconds. The soft, lovely flesh of her creamy, butternut thighs made her own thighs twitch as she imagined what lay beneath the too short skirt. She found herself admiring Sara's fingers as they lay relaxed on her thighs, so neat and dainty, and she imagined taking them into her own hands, stroking and caressing them, placing them against her body, licking them and sliding them between her lips so she could suck and draw the lovely scent of Sara's body into her mouth. She could feel herself moistening between her thighs and became increasingly aware of an electric sexual tension in the car.

'We need to make a stop,' Sara said, without turning her head towards Leah.

'Where?' asked Leah.

'My place,' Sara told her. 'Is not far.'

Leah should have objected, but she had never seen Sara's apartment and found herself curious, wanting to know more about the enigmatic girl. She allowed Sara to direct her, feeling the tension growing as they turned off onto a quiet side street and parked in front of an old brick apartment block. They both got out without exchanging words, and she followed the girl at a short distance, admiring her legs from behind as they entered the building.

'Is on the second floor,' Sara said, and walked up the stairs, Leah following, able to see up the short skirt which swayed around the tops of Sara's thighs as she moved, and felt a quiver of hunger in her stomach as she admire the girl's panties encasing her neat bottom.

It was an old building, and a wave of stuffy air drifted out into the hall as Sara opened the door to her apartment. Leah followed her in and looked around. It was a small apartment, typical of older homes that were subdivided into apartments. A new partition wall had been put up, reducing the size of the living room but creating a single bedroom and a tiny bathroom. The kitchenette was to Leah's left, separated from the front room by a small breakfast bar.

Sara moved into the living room and looked about almost nervously.

'Is something wrong?' Leah asked.

'No, why?' the girl asked, almost too quickly.

'Because you're acting strangely,' Leah told her, and then watched in amazement as Sara responded by removing her blazer to show Leah the lovely sight of her small but beautiful breasts pushing tautly against the white blouse she wore.

'Um, are you trying to taunt Mbweni?' Leah asked, feeling extremely flustered, reluctantly tearing her eyes away from the mouthwatering sight and looking up at Sara's sparkling eyes. 'Because I'm pretty sure she's not the type to tolerate such behavior.'

'You don't think I look sexy?' Sara asked, turning side on and running her hands up and down her body.

'That's not the point,' Leah said, even more confused, her mouth suddenly dry. 'You can't dress like that while on duty.'

'What if I playing role for decoy perhaps?' Sara suggested.

'Well, I suppose... but you're not.'

'No?' She let her hands slid up the sides of her brief

67

skirt, lifting it slightly to show her panties. 'I see the way you look at me, Leah,' she suddenly said, pointedly, catching Leah off guard.

'E-excuse me?' Leah stammered, blushing at being caught out so easily.

'I know you want me.' Sara began to slowly unbutton her blouse, then when they were all undone she seductively peeled her blouse off her shoulders, and Leah felt her heart skip a beat at the vision of her lovely naked breasts and erect nipples.

'Don't be silly,' she said, but with little conviction, reeling with excitement at the prospect of what Sara appeared to be offering, yet at the same time confused and wary about why she was behaving in such a way. 'What's got into you?' she asked, trying but failing to hide her interest.

Sara rolled her hips seductively and her tongue slid suggestively across her lower lip. 'What got into me?' she said, with a throaty chuckle. 'A lot got into me.' She reached to her right hip and undid the catch of her skirt, then slid the zip down and let the skirt slide down around her ankles.

'Sara,' Leah said anxiously, 'put your clothes on.'

'But I don't want to,' Sara said. 'I want to feel your body against me.' She stepped free of the discarded skirt and moved closer, Leah edging back warily.

'You know you want me,' Sara breathed, her eyes strangely haunted.

'No,' Leah denied, 'I... I don't.'

Sara reached out for her and Leah caught her wrists to block the touch, but the Asian girl immediately drew her arms back, pulling Leah's hands with them, which she swiftly caught and twisted, and before she realized it Leah found her fingers firmly cupping Sara's warm breasts, and a shudder ran through her body. She felt a wild thrill of excitement in the pit of her tummy but desperately fought against it and shrank back, falling across the sofa. Sara was instantly upon her, straddling her body, her hands cupping Leah's head, her body swooping down as she pressed her lips firmly against Leah's, her tongue thrusting between them. Leah grasped the girl's shoulders, but instead of pushing her away she squeezed them, then stroked, and despite her shock at the unexpected attack her tongue began to respond, to push back against Sara's as her body awoke with sexual electricity. She caressed the girl's smooth back, and melted into the long kiss with passion.

Instinctively Leah's hands slid down onto the girl's rounded bottom, kneading her buttocks, pulling her hips to hers. Sara cupped Leah's breasts, squeezing them through the thin sweater, then gently tugging it out of her trousers and pulling it up. She folded down her bra and cupped her breasts, squeezing them avidly, and then one delicate hand crept down Leah's belly and managed to edge beneath the waistband of her trousers, into her panties. She complained weakly as Sara's fingers found her sex and teased her clitoris.

With her free hand Sara managed to remove Leah's jacket, lift her sweater up over her head and drop it to the floor, then unclasping the bra she lowered her mouth and suckled her sighing colleague's nipples. Then her free hand lowered and undid Leah's trousers. She slid back to kneel on the floor between Leah's feet, pulling the trousers with her, removing them from Leah's long legs and discarding them on the floor beside her. Then she leant forward between Leah's legs, gripping her thighs strongly, forcing them back and further apart as she mouthed her sex through her black thong, her tongue lapping across the silk.

'S-Sara,' Leah gasped, but the Asian girl ignored her,

removing the thong and squeezing her face tight between her thighs again. Leah was overwhelmed with longing as she felt the girl's delicate mouth against her sex, as silken hair caressed her thighs.

Then Sara unexpectedly drew back, leaving Leah feeling cold and empty. Sara stood and went to the small desk just behind her, lifting a pair of handcuffs from one draw and turning, breathless, her eyes wild. 'Put these on me,' she demanded, her voice husky. She passed them to Leah, then turned and crossed her wrists together behind her back.

This was madness, Leah thought dreamily. They were supposed to be working, investigating a very serious case. But at that moment she didn't care. She rose to her feet, took the handcuffs, appreciating the feel of the smooth metal like she never had before, then gripped one of the Asian girl's slender wrists and snapped the cold steel around it. She felt Sara shudder, then took her other wrist, drawing it to the first, slipped the unyielding steel bracelet around it and clicked it locked.

Sara's arms pulled against the cuffs, then she turned, her breasts rising and falling rapidly, and sank to her knees before Leah. She leaned close again and Leah, in an increasing daze, reached down to run her fingers through the girl's silky hair, and sighed as she felt Sara's tongue slide between her sex lips, and could barely manage a coherent thought as she gripped the girl's pigtails, parted her feet a little more and ground herself against the pretty face between her thighs.

She'd never had any kind of a sexual relationship with another woman and never, until meeting Mbweni, seriously considered one. But now, with barely a doubt in her mind, she pressed the young Asian girl's face to her and moaned with pleasure as her tongue lapped her bare slit. 'Oh, *yes*,' she gasped in a choked voice.

Her hips rolled, grinding, her head lolling back. She tugged on the girl's pigtails, her knuckles white against the soft black hair as she forced the kneeling girl to greater efforts, felt the wet tongue sliding between the lips of her sex and flitting against the entrance to her vagina. 'Yes...' she whispered, her head back, her body straining, her legs apart as she drew the girl closer still.

She pulled on her hair, as if trying to draw the young Asian as tight to herself as she could, yet Sara made no complaint, licking and sucking her labia, then thrusting her tongue deep into her quivering pussy, and Leah's legs turned to rubber and she slumped back down onto the sofa behind her.

Sara fell with her, her mouth locked to her sex, and Leah sobbed with joy, her body writhing in helpless passion. Her legs lifted and wrapped around the girl's slight body as an orgasm flooded her and she began to shudder uncontrollably.

Then Sara was upon her, her soft flesh molding against Leah as they kissed, sucking and licking, their tongues dancing hungrily together. Leah rolled over on top of the handcuffed girl, nibbling the nape of her neck, then down to her breasts.

Breathless, she ran her hands over the other girl's breasts, swooning at her rigid nipples. She ran her fingers across them, and then bent and kissed them, sucking and licking, gently nipping with her teeth as Sara moaned and shuddered. Her hands moved adoringly up and down Sara's lithe body, and her thoughts swirled as she sifted through the differences between caressing a man and a woman.

Sara was soft, of course, her unblemished skin hairless, without the hard tendons and muscles a man possesses. Leah's hands followed the contours of the Asian girl's

71

lovely body, reveling in the smooth curves of her breasts and hips, the sweep of her trim waist, then gliding down between her thighs where, with barely a hint of hesitation, she palmed and squeezed the girl's pussy before rubbing her fingers against the wet lips.

'No, wait,' the girl moaned. 'Wait, please.' Leah released the nipple from her mouth and watched the girl look to the side. She followed her stare but didn't understand her meaning. 'In the desk drawer, please,' Sara begged.

Leah shakily got to her feet and crossed the floor. She opened the top drawer of the desk and saw a black dildo attached to straps lying within. Shocked, but wickedly excited, she turned to see Sara watching her. The girl looked oddly anxious and wary, yet at the same time afire with excitement.

'Use on me,' she whispered, 'please.'

Leah hesitated a moment, but then put the unfamiliar device on, drawing the straps up between her thighs and round her hips, then, a little dazed but wildly aroused, she gripped the dildo in one hand.

'Please use on me,' Sara pleaded again, and despite her indecision about whether she wanted or should take this step, Leah simply couldn't resist her.

She moved back to where the handcuffed girl lay on the sofa, and Sara spread her legs, drawing her knees back. Leah knelt on the sofa and gripped the thick plastic cock, rubbing it up and down against the moist opening of the girl's pussy.

'Hard,' Sara whispered. 'Use on me hard as you can. Use me like a whore.'

A shudder ran through her, and Leah pressed the nose of the thing down harder, feeling Sara's soft flesh give way before it, feeling some resistance as she dipped it in and pulled back, then pressed in deeper.

'Fuck me,' Sara implored, her passionate voice cracking slightly as she stared up at the lovely girl leaning over her, and Leah sank the dildo deeper and the girl gave a gasp of pleasurable discomfort.

'Are you okay?' Leah whispered.

'Harder, please,' Sara beseeched.

Leah drew back and thrust in, putting her hands down against the back of Sara's legs, forcing them down with her weight as she held herself above the slighter girl. She lowered her hips and Sara writhed as the dildo sank into her body.

'Are you okay?' Leah whispered.

'Yes, fuck me,' Sara responded breathlessly, and Leah did, instinctively settling into a rhythm, her taut buttocks lifting and sinking repeatedly, the supine girl's juices squelching audibly around the stout plastic length as it filled her cunt. Leah thrust deep and the girl cried out for more, Leah experiencing an intense sense of power and strength, wondering if this was how men felt when lovemaking.

Then she felt Sara's body begin to quiver and twist beneath her, and felt her own orgasm beginning to approach, gasping in time to Sara's gasps, and the two of them locked together in a massive climax, their bodies and voices joining in a chorus of mutual bliss.

Much of the rest of the morning was a blur of exquisite sex. Leah lay sprawled back on the sofa, her mind floating amid a sea of pleasure, pleasure which rolled over her in waves as Sara knelt between her legs, gently coaxing her through climax after climax.

Then in the shower later, their bodies slick with soap, they again enjoyed each other intimately. And then afterwards, both feeling replete and pleasantly drained,

Sara seemed bashful, more than a little awkward and embarrassed and eager to be dressed and out of her apartment.

They drove in silence to the first address on their list and Leah gradually felt ashamed of herself as well, feeling a sense of disbelief at what they'd done together, and her annoyance with herself and her confusion instilled in her a short temper with the men she interviewed, especially whenever they cast a lecherous eye at her lovely Asian colleague.

Chapter Five

Perhaps it was the bright light of the shop's fitting room, for Leah gazed at herself in the mirror and was filled with a sense of wicked excitement and shocked disbelief that she was actually considering buying, much less wearing the dress in public.

A week earlier she'd never have considered wearing such a garment. It was made of a shiny gray lycra, very tight across her breasts with a plunging cleavage line revealing the firm inner slopes of her breasts, and two thin halter straps. The hemline was very short, the skirt split almost to the hip on one side. It was a very sexy dress, as thin as silk and molded to her curvaceous figure. It was a dress for a sexy girl to go clubbing in, a girl who wanted to be seen, to be lusted after, to be desired.

And that had never before been Leah. Like all girls she liked attracting men's approval, appreciated and was flattered by male interest, when it wasn't unwanted or made too obvious. But she didn't like to be stared at or drooled over.

And if there was such a thing as 'fuck me' shoes, then the silver-gray five-inch heels she wore were they.

Leah's hands moved slowly up and down her body as she stared at herself in the mirror, transfixed. What would they think of her at the station if she showed up dressed like this?

Her fingers slid up through her hair. She was hot; she looked hot, and seductive. Any man would want her. She reached behind her neck and undid the halter string there, then eased the mini-dress down over her hips, stepping out of it, naked.

It had been a long and strange day, and she tried not to dwell on what had happened between her and Sara. She felt embarrassed every time she did, but worse than that, she felt a shameful excitement, too, which she tried to shy away from.

She thought back to the afternoon, to the eyes of the men she had interviewed, to the way they looked at Sara, their lusting so obvious to her that she wanted to slap them. And Sara basking in it, so smug as she played up to them, as she teased them with suggestive words and poses, pretending ignorance of the slavering eyes upon her. Leah had felt such strong urges to admonish the flirty little tramp, or even to take the little bitch across her lap and spank her bottom for her. She didn't, or course, but at one point as they left one building she did surreptitiously slap her bottom hard enough to make the girl yelp indignantly and blush, looking around hastily to make certain no one had observed the little chastisement.

Leah had to go and see Morales again, but she couldn't do so with such an intense sexual need still gripping her, or the meeting would surely end in only one way – and she didn't want to risk letting her defenses down like that again. She had been so stupid before and the thought of what might have happened to her was terrifying.

Having bought the dress she dropped the box containing it into the trunk of her car and drove home. She was not very hungry, but she put a readymade dinner for one in the microwave anyway. She went to her bedroom and crawled fluidly onto the bed for a few minutes, just to rest and have a little quiet time to herself.

The microwave pinged and her dinner was ready, so

she sighed and slipped off the bed, returning to the kitchen. She took the dinner out and spooned it onto a plate, fetched utensils and condiments, then sat at the table and ate, without too much enthusiasm, feeling almost grateful when the phone rang and she had an excuse to eat no more of the convenient but dull meal.

'Hello?' she said into the receiver.

'Detective MacInnes,' a familiar male voice stated.

'Lieutenant Bradfield?'

'You did not file your report on your interviews today, detective,' he said irritably. 'There's a high degree of pressure on this case. Perhaps you missed that point.'

She sat back on the sofa. 'Sorry, I apologize, lieutenant,' she said. 'I thought Detective Yi was doing that.'

'Well she didn't,' he snapped, 'and in my opinion the responsibility falls to you, detective.'

'Yes, I'm sorry, lieutenant,' she said again. 'But nothing we learned appeared to have any relevance to the case.'

'You are not the judge of that,' he said, clearly annoyed. 'You and your junior colleagues are merely the eyes, the ears and the legs. It is your superiors who are the brains, who piece information together.'

She slumped in frustration on the sofa. 'Yes, lieutenant, of course, lieutenant,' she said, her tone and attitude slightly offhand. Miserable old bastard, she thought.

'I will expect your report first thing in the morning, detective,' he insisted. 'And be grateful I don't order you to come in now and do it.'

'Yes, lieutenant,' she said, 'whatever you say, lieutenant.'

'Very well,' he said gruffly, concluding the conversation.

'And goodbye to you as well, you asshole,' she said to the dial tone, then she hung up, poking her tongue out at the phone, and standing she went back to her bedroom, lifting her new mini-dress from the box on her bed with intense reverence and awe.

She'd worry about the paperwork later; tonight she needed to release some stress; tonight she was going out for some fun!

Leah moved slowly through the hot club, the thumping bass of the music pounding all around her. People danced, crowds shuffling in the semi-darkness. A male face occasionally caught her gaze, eyes brightening until she moved on. She dodged a stumbling pair of laughing drunks, and then sidled through a group of men standing near the bar, looking for a drink.

The sensual fabric of the dress caressed her upper thighs, the slit up the side taunting ogling eyes as it opened and closed as she moved. Women gazed at her, assessing, comparing, sometimes intrigued, sometimes disapproving. Men stared, smiling appreciatively, licking lips, narrowing eyes, wanting her, commenting to each other as they eyed her, their lurid desires transmitted so obviously to her, what they wanted to do to her, what they wanted her to do to them. And she felt deliciously cruel, for she silently promised them the fulfillment of their desires, but she would give them nothing but a tantalizing vision to remember and regret never possessing. And it was desperately exciting to behave in such a provocative, seductive manner, as if something long forbidden were now freed from societal and professional disapproval.

At the bar a man bought her a drink, leering, eyes filled with hunger for her. She chatted idly, demurely, gazing about, feeling his hand sliding down her arm to her hip, then round to cup her bottom. With an alluring smile she slipped away from him, moving further along the bar.

A hand caught her wrist and guided her away from the bar a little. He was tall and arrogant looking, his face filled with smug self-assurance as he held her hips, walking backwards into the midst of the heaving, dancing throng. Normally she'd have reacted and had him on his knees in a flash, gasping in pain and begging for release. But now she followed obediently, her mind drifting a little, waiting to see what happened.

She began to dance with him, and that frenetic energy which had filled her body and mind for the past week surged to the fore as she rolled her hips and moved to the music. Her experience with Sara was still heavy on her mind. She had allowed herself to be seduced by the girl, right out of the blue. It wasn't as if she could excuse herself to giving in after a long period of flirting and coaxing by the lovely Asian. It just happened and Leah allowed and savored it. She'd just melted, and she was doing the same now, without a thought for the consequences, knowing she might let this stranger do anything he wanted to her.

What she'd done with Sara and what she might do later this evening was too much like what she'd felt with Morales, and too much like the bizarre dream she'd had about being tied and fucked from behind by some phantom on her balcony. And with Sara it had happened with someone she knew, someone she worked with. She didn't try to explain Sara's own conduct; Sara was a wild child and she knew that. But understanding why she had given in to her was much more troubling. She was going to have to confront Morales, because somehow, in some way she couldn't understand, he was responsible for the way she was behaving.

She brushed aside the thought that what she was wearing was a part of her strangely changed behavior. The hem of the short dress swayed seductively around her thighs as she swung her hips, and her swollen nipples strained against the tight clutch of the thin lycra, her breasts moving freely beneath it as she twisted and writhed to the rhythms of the music, and she was intensely aware of wearing nothing beneath. Nothing. And that thought did not petrify her as it would have not so long ago. But she did feel deliciously anxious every time she raised and entwined her arms above her head and felt the hem rise too, giving her a heady sense of danger. She'd never been an exhibitionist, but now the thought of strangers glimpsing more of her than perhaps they should only helped raise the heat of her desire. She felt wild and wanton, and it wasn't so much a matter of whether she would let someone from the club fuck her, but who, and how wickedly exciting that felt.

And then her dance partner was melting away into the heaving mass of sweating bodies as another man moved in to take his place. She felt a mild sense of irritation that the first man would give her up so quickly, so easily, but the last look she glimpsed on his face before the shadows and writhing bodies engulfed him was bewilderment, and she turned and looked at the man now dancing with her, and found her eyes falling into his.

'Did you know you were marked?' he said in a soft, throaty whisper that she somehow heard easily over the loud pulse of the music. She stared at him, her movements gradually slowing until she stood motionless amongst a frenzy of gyrating limbs. He drew her arms back, leading her towards a dark corner of the dance floor.

'What?' she said finally. He moved against her, his body molding to hers as he moved slowly to the music, catching every third beat to make it a slow dance, grinding his pelvis against hers as his arms slipped around her. His hands slid down to her bottom and squeezed, drawing her in harder against him, and Leah felt a wild thrill rolling through her body. She could feel him hardening against her as they danced, their eyes locked, their limbs moving almost instinctively, following the rhythm of the music.

She felt herself falling into his eyes, a breathless sense of anticipation and heat seeping through the pores of her skin as their bodies ground together. Her nipples ached as they pressed against his chest, and her lungs felt tight, her breasts swelling with arousal. His hands slid beneath her short skirt, lifting it, caressing her soft, overheated flesh. Another thrill staggered her as his palms made contact with her flesh, and another as she thought of others watching them. His lips found hers and she moaned into his mouth as his tongue thrust down against hers.

His hands skimmed lightly across the surface of her bottom, then pressed in more strongly, fingers kneading her buttocks, sliding firmly and hungrily over her skin, cupping her, forcing her legs wider, grinding his erection against her as couples moved around them and the music thumped.

Lights flashed through the darkness around them: green, blue, white and red, as they twisted through the gyrating bodies.

She felt him sliding the hem higher, and she was jerked out of her erotic reverie by the realization that he'd lifted the back up past her hips, the front following, and that anyone who looked would be able to see she was naked beneath. Shock flooded her but the dress was still moving, rucked up around her breasts, lifting her arms, sliding up over her head and off.

Naked but for her high heels she froze, stunned, her mouth open as though she wanted to protest but couldn't. He dropped the dress and seized her again, still dancing, pulling her naked body against him as they turned and twisted as one. The other dancers continued to writhe and move around them as if seeing nothing out of place.

His lips met hers, crushing down, his tongue thrusting between them as his hands stroked up and down her back and down to squeeze her buttocks again. Together they turned and turned again, brushing against the other dancers. She trembled with a shamefully intense lust burning within her lower belly. She pulled her head back, staring around; unable to understand what was happening and why no one was reacting. A harsh grip on her hair tugged her head back and she cried out in pain, but his lips muffled the sound as they again crushed firmly against hers.

They danced as if in a dream, and Leah's body continued to move to the music, her nipples, rigid and straining, raw and sensitive, rubbed against the harsh fabric of his blazer, sending flickering sensations of exquisite pleasure through her breasts.

She was naked! It couldn't be! Why wasn't anyone seeing? Was it all another bizarre dream?

She moaned as he cupped her breast and squeezed, as his fingers twisted in her hair and forced her head back. He growled as he bit into the sweep of her throat, and she bucked and trembled as pain flowed through her, doused an instant later by an even more consuming sexual hunger. Her hips ground repeatedly against him and she arched her back, whimpering in overheated confusion.

He turned her, lifting her right arm high, grinding himself into her buttocks as he bit the nape of her neck, and then, finally, through half glazed eyes, she saw someone who did not ignore them. He was a tall man with dark eyes, and he strode slowly towards her as her hips rolled and she trembled to the sharp prick of his teeth against her throat.

The newcomer began to dance, his hips moving in time

to theirs, his fingers sliding through her hair as his face grew nearer, his eyes enormous. His hands moved down her shoulders, down her sides to her hips, and his body pushed in, his groin rubbing against her moist sex. He too was hard beneath shining vinyl trousers and she gave a sob of helpless excitement as he leaned in to run his tongue down the other side of her throat.

His hands slid down and round to her buttocks, pulling her hips in against him, while the other man's hands eased down onto her breasts, squeezing her back. Their lips and tongues ravished her throat as the three rocked to the pounding drums and clashing electric guitars.

Leah's head lolled, her vision filled with pulsating lights as her body was squeezed between the two. She felt fingers at her sex and opened her mouth to scream her pleasure as a finger pushed inside her. Then she was twisted around and she grunted as her body hit the wall heavily. The first man was against her, his hand fumbling at his zipper, and she stared at the wall of dancers over his shoulder. She felt his hand pulling up under her right buttock, forcing her leg up, and then she cried out as he entered her, thrust in hard and deep and painfully fast. His hips slammed against her, crushing her into the wall as his mouth continued to chew and lick and suck at her throat.

He was big, not as big as Morales, but very long and thick, and she moaned and writhed against him, her legs trembling as she felt the soft heat of his spongy head against her sex, felt it pushing inside her, forcing its way through the straining lips of her sex, and then driving remorselessly up into her belly. She let out a strangled croak of pleasure as he buried himself within her, as she felt herself squeezing down around his stout shaft.

A dream. It was only a dream. It had to be...

He began to stroke, fast and hard from the first movement, his cock moving easily in her flooded sex. A dancer stumbled briefly against him and moved on. A couple of girls giggled at a table not far away, looking past them. A black couple writhed energetically to the music just to Leah's right.

'Unggg!' she groaned, an aggressive thrust raising her briefly off her foot. And then his hands were beneath her buttocks as she wrapped her long legs around his body and he began to lift her up and down as though she were a weightless rag doll, her burning pussy riding violently up and down his rigid erection as her arms grasped around his shoulders and she pressed her breasts against his chest. 'That's so good,' she moaned dazedly. 'So good.'

He turned, moved, but she hardly noticed. Then he was sitting at a table occupied by another couple deep in conversation about environmental issues. Leah's feet touched the floor at last, and she gasped blissfully as she felt herself impaled on his steely shaft. He squeezed one of her breasts and lifted it to his mouth as she pushed herself up, riding him, grunting each time she took him deep, moving wildly and frantically. He bucked up to meet her, his thick cock slicing up between the moist lips of her sex and jamming deep into her lower belly.

She cried out as her hair was yanked back, her head twisted to one side. She stared up at the second man, almost forgotten but, she now realized, a twin to the first, with dark eyes she felt like drowning in. She ignored the pain as he forced her head back, still moaning as the man she straddled thrust up into her sex. Then she saw the man undo his zipper and take out his erection. She dropped her eyes and stared at it openmouthed. It slid forward, and she closed her eyes and shuddered as she felt it against her lips. She licked the head as it entered her mouth, then opened her eyes and moaned aloud as his shaft slid deeper.

'Face it, if we don't cut back on fuel emissions the greenhouse effect will keep getting worse and...' The couple sitting across from them seemed oblivious to their presence. It had to be a dream. It had to be a bizarre dream.

She moaned again as the sturdy cock slid over her tongue, filling her mouth. She felt a slap on her bottom and began to ride once more, the muscles in her thighs aching with her awkward use, but lifting her nevertheless only to drop her down again. Every deep penetration sent the intensity of the heat within her soaring. People moved all around them as the music pounded, but no one noticed as she rode one man's cock and sucked another.

The sitting man continued to lick and suckle her breasts each time she rose up, often biting them as well. Her breasts felt tender and raw from his teeth, yet swollen with heat and an incredibly intense tingling pleasure. Every time his tongue rasped across one of her nipples she felt an orgasm mounting.

The man standing next to her thrust sharply and she shuddered, her rhythmic rising and falling missing a beat as he nudged into her throat. Her eyes widened, then she trembled against him, staring at his abdomen as her face was pulled in against it, feeling his thickness filling her throat and stretching her lips. And then she felt his cock lurching and felt the rush of fluid sliding down her throat.

He pulled back with a grunt and she swayed weakly, her eyes unfocused. The man she straddled jerked her up and down and she moaned and fell against him, grasping his hair, crushing her lips to his. His tongue invaded her mouth, thrusting her own aside, sweeping around the inside of her cheeks. His fingers squeezed her bottom and lifted her higher.

She felt a hiss and looked down through glassy eyes to see his lips drawn back. He had strange teeth. That was all she thought at the time. Strange teeth. They looked like fangs, two sharp canines, and then she watched him squeeze her breast, watched the fangs close slowly against her nipple.

She felt a pinch, and then a sharp pain followed by a soothing sense of cool relief. He opened his jaw and she saw her nipple had been pierced. She blinked uncomprehendingly.

He bit into her other nipple and she whimpered and writhed, feeling the heat and pain and relief at the same time.

'Mark her again,' a growling voice behind her said.

The hands beneath her raised her higher still, lifting her to her feet so that she stood, legs straight, her sex against his mouth. She swayed and rolled and arched her back as his tongue lapped over her clitoris and wet it afire. She couldn't keep still, could not stop her hips from gyrating against him.

She cried out in dazed wonder, feeling his thumbs spread the lips of her sex, force back the hood over her clitoris. She felt a sharp prick against her swollen pink bud and then a sudden blinding pain; so swiftly gone, however, that she had time for only one shocked jerk of her hips before the relief flooded through her.

And then his mouth was nuzzling her sex again and she was going insane. Once more the man behind seized her hair, jerking her head, forcing her back to arch as his lips met hers and a hand crept round to squeeze her breast.

It was sheer ecstasy. It swept over her, an orgasm making her shudder deliriously, of such staggering intensity she felt as though she were being consumed by it, and she cried out in exultation. Her body was being consumed by the fire of her climax and her mind spun helplessly amid the gale of climactic pleasure.

Leah stared out at the milling crowd, feeling a sense of shame that bit deep into her mind and body. She tried to drop her eyes, to stare at her feet, but the heavy collar around her throat was cleverly designed to press up against the underside of her jaw, preventing her from lowering her head.

Her owner jerked on the leash attached to her collar and pulled her forward. Her face burned as they left the tent and walked out amidst the crowd. Insults in countless languages were hurled in her direction, sneers and taunts from faces filled with contempt. Her wrists pulled against the shackles behind her back and she fought to keep tears from her eyes as she was led amongst the mob.

She yelped and jerked as a hand groped her bare bottom, and then jerked again, and again, hands reaching out from all sides, groping and fondling, slapping and squeezing. She cried out as someone cruelly pinched her nipple, and staggered as a finger almost penetrated her anus. Hands pulled at her hair and spitefully hauled her head back, and all the while the remorseless pull on her collar forced her to stumble forward.

The crowd was dense, consisting of men and women in heavy robes. The women were completely covered but for their eyes, the men wore richly patterned robes and headdresses like nothing she had ever seen before. Naked, she was pulled along at the end of the chain to the centre of the town, where some guards kept a space open and she was led into it – to the stocks.

She protested weakly as two strong men seized and moved her before the ominous wooden frame. Her hands were unshackled but tightly held and she was bent forward, her neck and wrists placed in the three hollows in the rough crossbar as the top was closed down upon them, leaving her bent forward with her bottom and sex helplessly exposed to the mob. It also left her breasts swaying as a man read something from a scroll, announcing her sentence to the jeering mob, while behind Leah a group of men were separating from the crowd, moving into a rough line. Her legs were parted and then her ankles chained down, and she cringed mentally as she knew even deeper humiliation was to be heaped upon her.

A man in black moved before her. He called something out to the crowd, which heckled in response. He stepped back and drew out a long thin bamboo cane, which he swished dramatically from side to side as the crowd cheered. Leah moaned in fear as she realized his intent, then lost sight of him as he moved behind her.

She pulled against the stocks, but her head and wrists were immovably locked in place. She felt a gloved hand move over her rounded bottom, then fingers kneading the soft flesh. The crowd encouraged him with bawdy comments, and then the hand left her and for a long moment she felt nothing. She braced herself, quivering, and then heard the hiss as the cane cut through the air.

The crack of noise as it struck her bottom was followed an instant later by a terrible pain of an intensity she had never known before. She screamed as her bottom burned, a fiery line of agony cutting across her pale buttocks. The crowd cackled and cheered as she writhed in helpless pain, the sound of the cane sweeping through the air was lost in their ragged noise, and then another intense slash of fire exploded across her rump.

Her bottom burned terribly, and as another, and another, and another explosion of pain cut into her flesh she jerked and twisted and screamed, tears filling her eyes and spilling down her cheeks, blurring the image of the mocking crowd.

And then there was a final blow and a voice called out. Eager men shuffled forward before her and, gasping sniffling and sobbing, she felt rough hands on her hips and thighs, and then her sex. She was immediately penetrated by an eager erection, and bony fingers clutched her hips as one of them began to fuck her roughly. A leering, dirty villager gripped her long golden hair and twisted it up and back, and as she opened her mouth to cry out he stuffed his erection in, stretching her lips wide and easily silencing her.

The crowd held back, laughing, jeering, watching as the two men used her trussed body. The one before her thrust to the back of her throat, his fingers digging into her scalp, jamming her forward to meet his furious thrusts, and the man behind her jerked his hairy groin against her tender, scalded bottom. Yet as humiliating as it was she was relieved by the crude abuse, for surely it was better than the pain of the beating.

The rutting behind her stopped and the cock withdrew, but an instant later she was mounted again, and from the feel of it by another man. She felt a shameful excitement beginning to thrum in the pit of her tummy as the rigid organ plowed into her, and moaned against the groin of the man thrusting into her mouth, which filled with salty sperm as he withdrew, and she swallowed as the man merged back into the frenzied crowd and another hurriedly took his place. She made no effort to fight or resist as this newcomer fed his cock contemptuously into her vacated mouth. A third stranger was fucking her from behind now, his hands eagerly mauling her body, sliding round her torso to knead her breasts.

Her mind felt fuzzy as the groin of the stranger standing before her pummeled her face, as his cock slewed back and forth between her stretched lips and over her tongue, pumping roughly to the back of her throat as a dark part of her reveled in the rough abuse. She was growing more and more aroused, and moaned around the cock filling her mouth in wanton pleasure as she tried to grind her bottom back.

Another man mounted her and she shuddered as the sexual heat rose, as she hungrily devoured the cock in her mouth. The man withdrew, squeezing his cock and spurting over her face as he came, only to be replaced by another.

She was on the edges of a climax when the voice called out again, a wild ululation of a howl. The men moved back and she cringed with shame as the circle opened and she saw all those eyes watching her.

Then the cane cracked down across her bottom again and she screamed, and with the fresh abuse being heaped upon her she felt her eyes fill with tears and sobbed as the cane cut across her upraised bottom again and again and again.

Ten, she thought, the idea coming from nowhere. Ten strokes. That was how many there had been the first time. She did not know how she knew this, but she was quite certain of the knowledge. She clenched her teeth, gasping and sobbing as another blow and another cut across her bottom. The pain was raw, jagged, enough to make her wilt as its force battered her soul.

Six blows and her pale white flesh was, she knew, a mass of welted red, flaring and throbbing. Seven blows and her neck jerked painfully against the wooden stock. Eight and she screamed and thrashed. Nine and she whimpered and prayed for it to stop, blubbering and begging for mercy, hoping she could withstand the last blow. And then it fell, and her scream was part horror and part relief.

The voice spoke again and the men moved forward. She all but collapsed in the stocks, but strong male hands held her hips up, and then they were fucking her again, sneering at her as they drove their hard cocks into her sex and down her throat.

She heard the bawling of a camel in the distance, and the braying of a donkey. Dogs barked and children shouted to each other from beyond the massed crowd. She coughed and choked as erect penis after erect penis was thrust into her mouth and their semen spilled onto her tongue and down her throat, over her face and into her hair. Hands roughly groped her breasts and she felt herself rousing, a sense of martyred masochistic pleasure flooding her dazed mind. A part of her railed against it, snarling and twisting and fighting to no avail as sex heat flooded her body and soul.

She was going to climax, she knew. She fought desperately to resist, but knew it was only a matter of time, and very little time. The man behind her knew what he was doing as he fucked her with vigor.

But then that voice called out again and she waited in trepidation. The hands and cocks moved away, leaving her panting, gasping, nearly swooning with illicit yearning. Then the cane cut across her bottom again and pain flashed through her nervous system to sweep her clear of any sexual torpor.

She clenched her teeth and felt anger towards those jeering faces, but at the same time a hungry sense of masochistic glee as pain was forced upon her. The cane cracked and snapped and bit into her defenseless buttocks as she twisted in helpless response. Yet she did not cry out any longer, somehow finding reserves of strength to deny them their victory as her body jerked to the violence of the beating.

She counted the number of strikes and then the men swamped her again, and she could no longer stop herself. She came with a shuddering, bucking, twisting violence, her eyes fiercely clenched as the orgasmic seizure sent convulsions through her exhausted body.

And then, barely conscious, she was released from the stocks and carried a short distance away. She was held against an upright post, her ankles lashed to the base of it, and her arms lifted and bound to a wooden crosspiece.

A greasy, foul smelling man leered down at her and gripped one of her breasts in grimy, calloused hand. Rough fingers squeezed the nipple, and he gleefully presented a fearsome needle in his other hand. She watched, strangely transfixed, as the tip of the needle pressed against the side of her nipple, she felt an intense pain as it pierced the poor bud, and then it was through and out the other side.

Before Leah could really comprehend what he'd done to her he thumbed her pulsing nipple, then slipped a gold ring through it, and bizarrely it struck her that it looked quite natural there.

He gripped her other nipple, pinching and twisting it, and that too was pierced and ringed. He said something, a soft babble in her ears, then he dropped to his haunches and she felt his fingers pressing against the hood of her clitoris, pushing it back to expose her moist, swollen bud. His fingers squeezed and then pain made her scream. The crowd roared with appreciation, drowning out her pitiful pleas for mercy, and then the man straightened up.

They freed her from the post and the man attached a new leash to her, this one attached to the ring that now pierced her clitoris. Her wrists were shackled behind her back once again, and she was led stumbling and staggering back through the crowd, her clitoris burning as the leash pulled against it, her bottom afire from her punishment.

'Miss? Time to go, miss. Come on. Need a cab?'

Leah opened her eyes slowly, blinking cautiously. Her body felt drained, utterly exhausted. She raised her head only with enormous effort to see one of the club's thickset doormen standing over the table. The club was largely empty, the lights up and bright, the music stopped. Table sets were being put together, glasses and dirty ashtrays removed.

'Had a few, have we?' he went on. 'Come on, honey, on your feet. Do you know where you live?' He helped her to stand, and she wobbled on rubbery legs. 'Got a purse? Got money? Ah, here we are.'

She wasn't sure how she got into a taxi. She sat back, half dozing, until they arrived at her building. Then the cabby helped her out of the vehicle and helped unlock her door. He slid her purse over her shoulder and gave her a little push, then went back to his cab.

She moved like an automaton into the elevator, leaning against the wall up to her floor, then down the hall to her apartment. Once inside she barely got the door closed before sliding down the inside and sitting dazed on the floor, where she again fell asleep.

Chapter Six

It was daylight when Leah woke, the bright sun streaming through her living room window. She raised her head and rubbed her shoulder where she'd been propped against the wall.

What on earth had happened to her?

She tried to stand up on legs painfully numb with pins and needles, wincing with the discomfort and effort, and after several failed attempts she succeeded, shuffling around on the spot for a minute or two until the blood flowed again and the feeling returned to her limbs, which for a short while only increased the pain in them. She held her head, her first thoughts that someone must have drugged her, perhaps tried to feed her one of the date rape drugs making the circuit of the clubs. If so, then whatever the scum had planned had failed. She remembered that she'd lost consciousness in the club, and the slime-balls must have been too frightened to try and take her out.

And then the dreams came back: stark, clear, and terrifying. But she was too drained to try and make any sense out of them and… something felt alien between her thighs, so with a growing sense of desperation she lifted the short hem of her dress and shrieked with shock. Her panties were missing and unbelievably her sex mound was shaved, and there was a small gold ring dangling from her clitoris! She stared, her mouth and eyes wide with astonishment, utterly unable to believe what she saw. Her fingers reached down very gently and touched her naked sex lips and the new adornment, and she gasped at the incomprehensible rush of excitement it caused.

It wasn't possible. She had only gone to a club. She had lost consciousness but woken – admittedly somewhat worse for wear – still in the club. She had definitely not gone anywhere else with anyone else. She remembered the sharp canines of one of the two strangers, remembered them closing around her nipples, and remembered the pain as he then buried his face between her legs.

Frantically she struggled out of her dress completely and stared down at her nipples, neatly pierced, thin gold rings the diameter of quarters dangling from each. In disbelief she pressed her fingers against her nipples and their new lodgers, rubbing them lightly and quizzically, still unable to believe her eyes. As with her clitoris, her nipples were even more sensitive than usual.

This wasn't possible. Leah had actually considered getting a nipple pierced once, years earlier. She considered it strongly enough to actually look into what was involved, and the literature spoke of weeks of healing and discomfort, especially for a genital piercing. Yet she reached down and fingered her clitoris again, trying to ignore the rush of pleasure it brought her, feeling no sense of pain or soreness at all.

'It's not possible,' she said in awe, also wondering how she came to have a denuded sex. And people did not come with fangs. Teeth like those the two seducers in her dream possessed were the stuff of B-movies and nightmares.

She jerked her head up and her hand rose to her throat. She hurried, naked, into the bathroom and leaned forward across the basin to stare at her reflection in the mirror. She raised her chin and scanned her throat, and incredibly tiny twin punctures, a little like insect bites but larger, marked the flesh. But how could that be? It had all been a weird dream, surely.

She struggled to come up with an explanation. Perhaps they *were* insect bites. They had to be.

Her attention moved back to the gold rings piecing her nipples, and looking at them in the mirror she fingered one, carefully turning it, actually enjoying the strange sensation as it moved through her stiffening bud. She searched for the clasp, but she was stunned to discover it had none. And that wasn't possible, either.

Her fingertips slid around and around the thin gold ring, searching for a break, for any kind of line that would indicate how it opened. She lifted it, trying to see better, wincing as it pulled on her nipple. But there was no join, no way she could see of removing it, and it was the same for the other two.

She had never considered a clitoral piercing, though she had read up on them a little. Most piercings were through the labia or at worst the hood over the clitoris. Doing the clitoris itself was considered too dangerous, for if anything went wrong it could cause a lack of sensation, or worse. That clearly had not happened here. Not only was her clitoris pierced but there appeared to be nothing to indicate it had been recently done, neither soreness nor blood. And she was clearly just as sensitive as always, if not more.

She had to sit down on the toilet and spread her legs, then use a mirror to examine the ring better. It was nearly a twin of the others, but a little smaller, and like them it had the weight to be a constant reminder of its presence. In fact, though smaller and just as thin, it appeared even heavier than the two piercing her nipples.

As her fingers caressed her inner thighs she gazed in wonder at her naked sex. She had once experimented with shaving between her legs and not liked the results. Yet this was something entirely different. There was no soreness, no redness, and no stubble, nor even the hint of any. Her fingers gently traced the lips of her sex, then up and down in widening circles, and found nothing but smooth, soft, clear skin.

She stood up again and stared at herself in the mirror. Her sex was more obviously visible than she remembered seeing it since she'd been quite young, and the ring through her clitoris seemed to glint proudly from between her labia. She drew in a sharp breath, the fingers of both hands moving distractedly across her sex. What the hell had happened to her?

Leah spent several hours pacing back and forth, naked all the while, trying to understand what had happened to her and considering what, if anything, she could do about it. Clearly there was no one she could talk to about it. There was no agency to which she could report, no group she could consult. She was alone, and had to deal with whatever was happening to her alone.

What had been done to her was frightening, yet she remained intrigued by it in many ways. It disturbed her that she could not remove the rings from her body, yet every time she saw herself in a mirror she felt a sense of breathless excitement. It worried her that her pubic hair had somehow been removed, but her pussy thrummed with simmering excitement at how lovely her naked sex looked.

And she was aroused, not uncontrollably so, but her nipples tingled and her pussy was moist as she paced back and forth. The little rings were not heavy, but as she moved around her apartment they moved too, tugging at her stiff nipples and sensitive clitoris so that it took resolve to keep from touching herself, and a steely determination not to masturbate.

She decided to work off some energy by exercising, still naked. Something about the idea of putting clothing on seemed vaguely unnatural to her. And so she did her calisthenics, then jogged on her treadmill and lifted some weights, working out for over an hour until a faint sheen of sweat covered her body.

She then showered, and could resist her soapy body no longer, her fingers stroking her ringed clitoris, her free hand squeezing and kneading her breasts. The orgasm was immensely powerful and she sank to her knees on the tiled floor of the shower. She felt amazed at herself as she knelt there, knees spread, fingers thrusting desperately into her sex as she stroked her clitoris, the climax rolling over her again and again as she shuddered and moaned in helpless pleasure.

Afterwards she fell back against the shower wall and let the hot water rain down over her body, gulping in air. The power of the orgasm was greater than anything she had ever experienced... except for her experience at the nightclub, and the previous week with Morales.

How were they linked, she wondered, for certainly they must be?

And that gave her someone to talk to, to question, someone to tell her what had happened, what was happening to her. But first she would find out everything there was to know about Señor Morales.

Rodrigo Morales had no driver license. He had no social insurance number. He had no passport. He had no criminal record of any kind. None of the normal channels Leah used had any listing of the man. He did not, for example, even have a credit record, much less a credit card. So perhaps that was not his real name.

She examined her notebook and then called up the Land Registry on her computer, and much to her utter astonishment and disbelief there was no building at the address she gave for his residence. Nor was there a list of planning consent or building warrants from the local authorities, and a land use chart showed an empty space in the lot occupied by Morales' house. And yet the building had appeared to be very old – at least a century old, she judged. So how could it possibly have been missed?

Leah was still naked and still aroused, and doing her best not to touch herself. She was slouched down in her chair, her feet on the coffee table, the keyboard over her thighs doing much to prevent her hands from almost subconsciously sliding down to finger her sex.

She lifted the keyboard and sat up straighter, placing it on the table so she could stand. She was feeling hyper due to the sexual energy in her system. She padded into her bedroom and considered her options. For confronting Morales a business suit would be best. Yet something inside her rebelled at the thought, so instead she pulled on a lacy black thong and a pair of jeans. She tugged an old white halter that had shrunk in the wash over her shoulders, tugging it down over her breasts. The top showed a goodly portion of cleavage and left most of her midriff bare, and she ran her hands over her stomach, enjoying a quiver of excitement. The top was very tight, serving to support her breasts in the absence of a bra. Of course, it was also quite obvious to the casual viewer that not only was she not wearing a bra, but her nipples were erect, too. And an even closer view would allow the discerning eye to realize the presence of rings, as well.

She posed before her mirror, feeling the tingle in her nipples grow stronger as the soft cotton molded tightly to them. She shuddered and squeezed herself through the tank top, then slipped her feet into her shoes and headed down to the street.

It felt slightly wicked to be out in such gear in broad daylight. A woman who safeguarded her reputation, Leah had always been careful about what she wore, about what image she would present. But now she felt her nipples pulsing with excitement as she walked along the sidewalk to where her car was parked.

She walked as if in an enveloping cloud of sexual heat, aware of every movement of her body, of the dampness in her thong and the fullness of her breasts as they strained against the tight front of her top.

It was a short drive to Morales' home, and she parked against the curb and remained behind the wheel for a while, staring up at the house. It looked normal enough, though in daylight it seemed much older than she had thought. That only made it more bizarre that the house did not even appear on the local land registrar's maps.

And it was very disconcerting the way she had allowed him to do whatever he'd wanted to her in there. Why had she submitted to a complete stranger in such a way? She should have known better, and the fact that she should have known better but still let it happen really frightened her. What if she surrendered to him once again?

Who was he? *What* was he? She reached up and touched her fingertips to her tender throat. Legend spoke of the ability of vampires to cloud the mind, to seduce women…

But where the hell did *that* thought come from? What had he done to her? Was she going insane?

Flustered and anxious Leah got out of the car and walked quickly up the path to the front door, rapping on the knocker and ringing the bell before her wavering resolve could evaporate completely. Her heart pounded and her tummy fluttered in apprehensive anticipation as she awaited an answer that did not come. She rang again, and again, then looking around her, stepped off the porch and moved around to the rear, trying to peer through gloomy windows as she did.

She tried a door at the back more out of habit than any hope of it opening, but the latch turned in her hand and she froze as the door eased open a crack. With her heart beating quicker she inched it further open and peeked inside, spying a short hall with another door at its end. She slipped inside and closed the backdoor behind her, careful not to make a sound, and then crept up to the next one, which was unlocked too. She opened it slowly, and saw to her surprise a narrow set of wooden stairs doing down.

With apparently no other way in to the house she forced herself to make her way down the stairs. As she reached what she had thought was the bottom she realized the stairway only turned, and another flight led still deeper into the bowels of the house. Frowning, wondering why anyone would need a basement so deep, she continued down. Vampires, she thought, the silly thought coming from nowhere; they would want to be deep to be sure of avoiding any daylight. She tried to shake off the thought as absurd, but it persisted as she reached the lower level.

Now she was in a chilly narrow passage made of unpainted wooden boards. There appeared to be no doors, save for the one at the far end, and a single low voltage light bulb hung overhead illuminating her path as she continued, against all her instincts to turn and flee immediately, to that door.

Taking a deep breath to try and calm her trembling hand she turned the handle and pushed the door, and it opened onto more steps, these of stone. It was warm now, but she felt a chill run down her spine as she took each dusty step in turn, slowly and quietly. As before there was a turn and then more steps descending deeper and deeper, and as before, she emerged into a narrow passage, this one hewn from stone walls and a claustrophobically low stone ceiling.

It was cold again and she crossed her arms protectively, trying to warm herself in vain, the gloomy passage barely lit by flickering torches as she moved fearfully along it.

A heavy wooden door appeared through the murkiness ahead. Leah swallowed nervously as she reached it, and then lifted the heavy iron latch. With her heart thumping as adrenaline pumped through it, she slowly pushed the door open to find a circular stone chamber lit by two torches set in the damp walls. There were waist high animal cages set against the wall to one side, and as Leah slowly, anxiously eased inside, she saw, to her shock and horror, that there were girls locked in them.

The light was too dim to tell if they were the same girls they'd been trying to find during their investigation. And as one raised her head Leah found herself staring in fearful dismay. The girl had been shaved entirely bald, and she was nude. There were four of them, lying on their sides in the cramped cages like undernourished animals in a third world zoo. They each had a bowl of water and scraps of food, and she stared, appalled that someone would reduce healthy females to the status of caged beasts. Outrage swelled within her and she hurriedly opened the cages and let them out, whispering comforting words of encouragement, thinking they must be traumatized by their imprisonment and whatever perversions they had been subjected to.

'Come on, I'll get you out of here,' she assured them in anxious whispers. 'Don't worry, we'll be out of this shithole in minutes.'

The girls crawled out of their cages and rose onto unsteady legs one by one, and as the fourth was released Leah turned to stare at them, blinking in amazement. They were very nearly identical in their nudity, with firm breasts, shapely hips, narrow waists and slender legs. Their faces were nearly identical too, though they were not, she realized, the girls they were looking for. And their heads were perfectly smooth, not as if shaven, but more as if they had simply been born without hair.

Yet the most remarkable thing about them was their eyes, for all had alarmingly dilated pupils. She had never seen anything like it in her life, and for a moment she could only gape in disbelief.

And then she noticed, with an increasing sense of foreboding, that each girl had rings through their nipples, and that those rings were identical to the rings piercing her own. Her eyes dropped and she saw they were pierced through the clitoris too, and suddenly her mouth felt intolerably dry with fear and she struggled to swallow.

One of the girls shuffled closer, reaching for Leah. Leah gripped her wrists, fending off the fingers that twisted towards her face, but then the girl pulled back, drawing Leah's hands to her lips, licking her knuckles. Surprised and disturbed Leah yanked her hands away.

'Come on,' she said, her voice shaky, 'we have to get out of here.'

Another of the girls moved behind her, her arms creeping around Leah's waist, her full breasts molding against her back as she ran her moist tongue up her neck.

'Stop it!' Leah turned, twisting defensively and pulling away, staring at the girl in confusion and uncertainty. The backs of her fingers felt hot, and she rubbed them subconsciously against her jeans even as she reached up

103

with her other hand to rub her neck. 'We have to go,' she said more desperately, moving towards the door as she wondered what manner of psychological problems the poor girls had been condemned to. They were all beautiful, and despite their hellish surroundings and bizarrely bald heads they looked deeply sensual. In addition to the rings each girl had a silver band around her ankles and wrists, with a similar but slightly wider band encompassing their throats, an odd, unreadable inscription engraved into them, possibly in Arabic.

Again one of the girls grabbed Leah from behind, her hands cupping her breasts as her deceptively strong arms hugged her.

'Dammit!' Leah cursed, wondering what was up with them. Why didn't they just follow her out of that hellhole as quickly as they could? Surely they were desperate to escape?

Another of the girls dropped to her knees in front of her and gripped her hips, then leaned forward, lapping at her bare belly, her tongue indulging long slow laps across Leah's soft skin. 'W-we have to get out of here!' she gasped despairingly, trying to shake free of them. But they were quickly all over her, the other two girls gripping her wrists, drawing her hands up to their lips, and they began to suck and lick her fingers as Leah struggled with increasing fear, frustration and confusion.

And more. For some inexplicable reason she was becoming increasingly, helplessly turned on. The simmering sexual warmth that had lurked all day was still present when she'd found the girls, but that was nothing compared to the furnace building within her now. It was not natural and not acceptable, she kept trying to tell herself that, but she felt almost drugged in her physical and mental responses. One of her hands felt like it was burning, the skin raw, the nerve endings flaring with power, and somehow she realized that this was where the first girl had licked her. And then she realized her neck felt the same, and that she was feeling intense sensations everywhere the girls were licking, as if their saliva was somehow setting her skin aflame.

'Let me... let me go!' she gasped, twisting and struggling, but her arms were drawn out to the sides, the two girls holding them licking up and down their length. The girl kneeling before her had slavered hungrily over her naked tummy, and her hands were now undoing her jeans.

'*No*,' Leah gasped, struggling with growing desperation, 'please no. I'm trying to help you. Please, we must get out of here!' Despite her fraught pleas for commonsense to prevail she felt her jeans being tugged down, and with them her delicate thong, and the realization came to her that if their saliva did somehow contain some type of chemical enhancement she did not want them anywhere near her... '*Noooo...*' she implored as the girl's mouth pressed avariciously between her thighs.

Leah's hips rolled in shocked dismay as the girl's tongue thrust impossibly deep between her labia, wriggling deep inside her vagina, probing and twisting and then withdrawing to flit teasingly around her clitoris. She couldn't comprehend what they were doing to her. She was only trying to help them, risking her own safety for them, but they seemed to totally disregard that and far from desperately scrambling to escape this macabre hell, they were effectively raping her instead. Her tight top was being tugged up and off and her struggles became increasingly confused and feeble as she tried to fight the creeping lethargy and intensity of sexual need sweeping her mind and body.

'I d-don't want you to do this to me,' she begged, conflicting need and loathing vying for supremacy, but they disregarded her, their expressions fixed with emotionless determination as their tongues lapped her shoulders and throat, her fingers and the palms of her hands. She sagged to her knees and the girls gathered her body into theirs, hands mauling her breasts and buttocks and thighs. She swayed weakly, her hips beginning to roll with the raw need blossoming within her.

Their tongues stroked her flesh, and everywhere they touched heat flared. Her skin began to feel raw and exquisitely sensitive, and she rolled her head weakly, arching her back as the two before her mouthed her breasts and suckled her nipples.

Feeling defeated and overrun she sagged lower on her knees, and rolled her head forward to see, dazedly, that one of them had slid beneath her parted thighs and was gazing up at her silently, waiting, and despite the last fragments of her determination to resist the onslaught, Leah surrendered and sank down onto her waiting mouth and let out a shocked cry of pleasure as the girl's tongue thrust up between the lips of her sex, wriggling deep within the tightness of her body, stroking wetly across her clitoris.

'Oh, *no*,' she panted, in futile denial of the dangerously delicious attention.

Another girl knelt behind her, her tongue sliding slowly, wet, hot down her spine. Leah's hips writhed, and then the girl's tongue was between her buttocks, probing at her anus, and she came, shuddering, her pelvis jerking helplessly. She moaned in wondering pleasure, swaying and sandwiched between the mass of writhing flesh and limbs.

Then she glanced up through lowered lashes and saw him there. A strong male hand gripped her hair, forcing her head back. She gasped, the pain minimal, drifting sparks amidst the furnace roaring through her. His eyes were intense, and she stared up into them. Then he released her and she drowned again amongst the other girls as he turned and left the squalid basement room.

Eight hands captured and caressed her body, lips and tongues bathing her in fire and lust. A sudden climactic shockwave sent her mind reeling, and for long minutes she rocked to the power of sexual bliss, her mind spinning and tumbling.

Her eyes seemed to clear a little, and then a strange desire gripped her. She lowered her hands, fingers searching, finding pussy lips, finding clits swollen with lust and adorned with gold rings. The girls shook violently, and almost as one their heads were thrown back, their lips wide, their eyes closed. Leah's fingers rubbed furiously across the swollen wet buds, and one delirious girl fell forward against her, shaking with convulsions, eyes closed tightly.

Then Leah fell back, hot female flesh covering her. The five of them rolled and writhed on the cold, grimy floor. Her mouth found another's and their lips mashed together, tongues squirming and thrusting. Her hips bucked wildly as she felt a moist tongue worming up into her anus. Fingers rubbed at her clitoris and pushed into her pussy, while tongues lapped at her toes and her breasts and her face and her throat.

She had no sense of time. She was exhausted, sweating, her muscles aching, her belly and breasts tight. Yet she could not break free. Every time she summoned her resolve and tried one or another of the frenzied girls would find a way to send her pulse soaring again.

After what seemed like hours of erotic overload Leah managed to pull partially free while the entwined mass of girls were occupied with each other. With sweat matting her fringe against her forehead she gripped one of the cages and dragged herself to her knees. Yet as if her movement had refocused their attention she felt their hands crawling up her calves and thighs.

Leah pushed at them, pushed at their upturned faces as they rose to lick her. With enormous effort she succeeded in dragging herself to her feet, but her legs were parted, straddling one of the girls, and her knuckles whitened as her fingers desperately grasped the top bars of the cage for support, and when a soft hand slid up to palm her sex she could only whimper and tremble.

Then there were two of them up with her, pressing their soft breasts against her arms as their lips sought her throat. She shoved one back. The girl stumbled, but her expression emotionless came forward again, reaching for her, fingers piercing her sex.

'N-no...' Leah sobbed shakily. More fingers pushed into her, and she twisted weakly between the two girls sandwiching her. Their tongues lapped her throat. Their hands cupped and kneaded her breasts. The pressure against her sex became unbearable, almost enough to distract her from the suffocating heat billowing around her. She tried to close her legs but felt strong hands gripping her ankles and thighs. 'Fucking b-bitches,' she gasped, teeth clenched.

Then the knuckles of the girl kneeling behind her were forced up between her taut pubic lips and Leah let out a gurgling cry of dark, terrible pleasure as she realized the entire hand had been squeezed into her pussy. She came with a helpless cry of wild passion, rocking and shuddering against them as the hand pushed deeper and deeper into the soft folds of her sex, fingers twisting like a live creature within her.

Her orgasm seemed unending as she felt the fingers curl in against the palm to form a fist. The fist pushed deeper, a living ball in her lower belly, twisting slowly as hands clutched her legs, holding them spread wide.

'P-please... please...' she gasped.

One of the girls sprawled on top of the cage, laying back, legs spread, drawing Leah's mouth against her wet sex as the fist began to pump slowly up and down in her aching belly. She grunted and moaned, her lower body pulled back as the fist withdrew, her thighs grinding against the edge of the cage as it pushed forward again.

She licked dazedly at the girl's wet sex, the scent of her almost narcotic, the taste of her even more so. She felt a fuzzy heat spreading on her tongue, filling her mouth and down her throat as the girl's juices flowed. She groaned as the fist moved more powerfully, her lower body grinding to and fro.

Warm lips agitated her clitoris and another orgasm rolled over her as she eased herself back on the balled fist inside her, the experience awful yet exquisite. She cried out with each deep impalement, but the intense discomfort did nothing to lessen the terrible, all consuming need, her breathing harsh and ragged. Another shattering orgasm tore through her mind and body and she screamed, heedless of who might hear, uncaring for anything but the ecstasy racing through her core.

Chapter Seven

Leah woke slowly, exhausted, her body aching in every joint, every muscle. She sat up slowly, holding a hand to her forehead, her hair spilling down around her shoulders. She opened her eyes, blinking slowly, her mind confused. She had no idea where she was, and for long moments she had no idea why she was wherever it was. Then it all fell into place and she gasped, jerking her head up and staring about her.

She was in her car, parked at a curbside. Morales' house was just ahead, brooding darkly in the shadows. She was nude, and there was no sign of the clothes she'd worn earlier.

She raised her hands then at a foreign sensation, staring at them. There were gold bands circling her wrists, and she saw looking down, two more circling her ankles. She ran her fingers around them but found no breaks, no clasps, no way of removing them. They were, she thought chillingly, the same as those the bald girls had worn. Was she to be made into one of them?

Her hands scrabbled frantically at the ignition and the motor turned over smoothly. She threw the car into gear and heard the tires squeal as she pulled out into the road, narrowly missing a car parked in front of her.

It was almost four in the morning by the clock on the dashboard, and the roads were empty as she raced through them, her mind reeling, fear clawing at her insides. What was Morales? He couldn't be a vampire; there was no such thing!

She began to slow at the lack of pursuit, feeling a growing sense of awareness at her nakedness, and how vulnerable it made her. She glanced hopelessly over her shoulder at the rear seat, knowing there was nothing there with which to temporarily clothe herself, knowing also that the trunk contained a toolbox and spare tire, and nothing more.

She kept to the quieter roads as much as possible as she returned to her apartment, then parked at the rear entrance, near the laundry, not wanting to make her way naked through the brightly lit garage.

There were no lights on in the nearby buildings, and few on in her own. Her heart was pounding and her ears were alive to every little sound as she slipped the key out of the ignition and held up the one to the building. She searched for but found no alternatives, so she opened the car door and stepped out, naked, into the night air.

Anxiety made her tummy churn, but there was more, a dark, crackling sense of heat rose around her at being outside, out in public, naked to the world. Fear of discovery made her tremble as she headed for the rear door, but the quick sprint she had planned turned into a slow, unhurried walk as a dark part of her gloried in her shameless nakedness, exulted in the sense of freedom. She felt almost as though she was in a dream, a part of her screaming at herself to run, but her legs refusing to comply.

Eventually the key turned easily and the door pulled open. She slipped inside, her feet slapping lightly on the floor tiles as bright fluorescent lights stripped away any sense of comfort the darkness had leant her. She drew a deep breath then, heart hammering, pulse racing, anxiety setting butterflies fluttering in her stomach, she crept along the hall to the elevators, her disquiet increasing at the thought of being discovered before she could reach the sanctuary of her apartment. She held her finger to the button and watched it glow, listened, barely able to hear over her pounding heart as the machinery engaged and the elevator dropped from above.

She stood still, waiting as the doors opened, then thankfully stepped in, turning and pressing the button for her floor. The elevator began to rise smoothly, and she stared as each floor number lit up in sequence, hardly able to breathe, and as each number lit and then went out as she ascended she felt a desperate sense of relief that the elevator hadn't stopped for someone to alight, only for that relief to be instantly replaced by fears that the next floor might be the one when it did.

Eventually she breathed a deep sigh of relief as she reached her floor, and a soft chime sounded as the doors opened and she padded out along the carpeted hall to her door. Unable to believe her good fortune in making it home safely she unlocked it and slipped gratefully inside.

Leah trembled as she leaned back against her closed door, and raised her hands again, staring in disbelief at the bands around her wrists.

She moved away from the door, rubbing her arms. She felt a sense of barely suppressed energy, felt hyperactive as she began to pace back and forth in front of her large glass windows. Her thoughts were in turmoil as she tried to explain away what she had seen, and what had happened to her. Morales was a cult leader of some kind, the others his followers. That much was surely clear and everything could be explained that way. And those two creeps in the nightclub were obviously, although it was a massive coincidence, part of the cult, wearing fake teeth and playing at being vampires.

Yet she could not explain away the uncontrollable,

heightened lust she'd felt almost constantly since first meeting Morales, and could not explain the fiery heat she'd felt burning through her flesh at the touch of the girls' tongues. She had to squeeze her thighs together as she recalled the moment one of them thrust her tongue into her quim for the first time.

She woke, eyes snapping open and staring at the wall opposite the foot of her bed. She lay on her side, curled up in a fetal position, one hand between her legs, her other cupping a breast. She slowly unfurled, rolling onto her back, letting the hand clamped between her thighs slide away, flopping lifelessly onto the mattress beside her as she stared up at the ceiling.

None of it was possible. None of it.

The afternoon sun streamed through the window, and she rolled out of bed. She showered, then dressed in a tight pale blue blouse, a short black leather skirt, and black leather boots with four-inch heels. It was hardly the proper attire for a police officer about to interview potential witnesses, but something inexplicable influenced her to make the choice, and made her slip into her favorite leather coat, the one she normally only ever wore for nights out.

Outside she got into her car, started the engine and pulled away from her apartment block. She tried to ignore the memories of what had happened to her in recent days. Morales. Somehow he had done things to her mind, to her body. But how could she fight him, much less his kinky entourage?

She paused as she spotted a church ahead, and turned in. She got out of her car but hesitated briefly, absurdly wondering if she were cursed, and if so whether she would be able to enter the sacred place at all. But she felt nothing as she passed through the large arched doorway, and a sense of relief filled her. For some reason she felt the need to make her way up the aisle, and halted at the small stone basin and gazed at the water within. Holy water. By all the legends and myths, holy water was a weapon to be used against... against vampires.

But what was this lunacy? Why was she even thinking this way?

She stared down at the water, and then tentatively put a hand out, fingers extended to brush the cool surface. She drew them back and made the sign of the cross over her chest, felt self-conscious as she stumbled awkwardly through a quick prayer, then turned and hurried out.

She had previously printed off a list of local shops supplying gothic clothing, accessories, books, comics and memorabilia, so she began to visit them one by one, asking the proprietors or staff for information about the vampire legend and whether they knew of any customers who may have thought such things really existed, showing pictures of the missing girls to see if anyone recognized them or whether they might jog some memories.

Most of the stores appeared to be little more than hobby shops for the terminally silly, for teenagers and goths and oddballs and cranks. There were a few aimed at Wiccans and the granola cruncher set, but they were little better. Almost all of them focused on witchcraft, love potions, and communicating with the dead; the mention of vampires drew blank looks or amusement.

It wasn't until she happened upon a shop in a seedy basement that she found anything of interest. The shop was tiny, the shelves and products on them handmade, and the proprietor a wizened old man with surprisingly bright green eyes, but at the mention of vampirism those eyes narrowed defensively and flickered up and down as if examining her anew.

'You'll not find much relation between petty potions and vampires, miss,' he said in a rasping voice. 'What all these would be magic users try to do at best, is imitate what some do natural like.'

'I don't understand,' Leah said.

'Well, not that I'd know of course, but if there was a vampire, not that I'm saying there is of course, but if there was you'd not find them messing about with potions and charms and ingredients for brews and such. According to myths and legends they have their own powers, powers that come natural, or as we might say, unnaturally to them. Powerful creatures are vampires, so they say.'

'And what powers do vampires possess, exactly?' she asked in a skeptical voice.

'Aside from the power over death, you mean?' he asked with a wry smile. 'Oh, unnatural lifespan, speed and strength, as all the movies show, and a powerful ability to influence what others think and feel. They say one could be standing right next to you and you'd not know it unless he or she wanted you to.'

'You mean that bespelling with the eyes nonsense?' Leah asked, getting more intrigued.

'Something such as that, but I think there's considerably more to it.'

'Such as?'

'Am I an expert on vampires and legends, or something?' he asked with a little laugh. 'Besides, if there was such a folk they'd not look happy at me talking about them to the police. Not at all.' He looked around and then slyly back at Leah. 'They'd not look happy at people poking around asking questions about them, neither.'

'I'm not terribly worried,' she said coolly, but with little conviction.

He smiled, somewhat sympathetically. 'You should be,

115

dearie,' he said. 'You should be.'

'Where could I find more information about them?' she asked, trying to shake off the sudden feeling of dread his sinister words provoked.

He sighed and shook his head. 'There are a few, um, practitioners of lore who might be willing to tell you a thing or two.'

At last Leah felt she might just be getting somewhere. 'Can you give me some names?'

The late afternoon seemed chilly as she left the shop, and she drew her coat closer about herself. The sun was setting, and she mentally scoffed at the thought that vampires would soon be out and about. Vampires, she thought scornfully; the idea was ludicrous. What she had come across was a cult, perhaps with some expertise in hypnotism or drugs.

She got into her car and glanced down at the first name on the list, then started the engine and pulled away from the curb, determined to find something out before returning home.

Leah felt blind for a long moment, or almost blind, for there was a small circle of light directly in front of her, off in the distance. She was cold, chilled and she groaned weakly as she tried to raise her arms. They seemed immensely heavy. Her back was aching and she had a blinding headache. Her vision swam, and then slowly came into focus, and she realized she was staring at a distant neon sign – an upside down neon sign.

No, she was upside down, or rather, her head was upside down, hanging over the edge of… something. Her head slowly cleared. She was sprawled spread-eagled across something, her legs hanging over one side, her head, shoulders and arms over the other.

She groaned as she struggled to right herself, wriggling downwards, grasping the sides of whatever it was and pulling herself back so that her shoulders and head no longer dangled. She pushed herself upright, which was a mistake, the rush of blood making her vision swim again. She fell back, hitting her head on whatever it was she was lying on. She felt and heard her stomach rumble alarmingly and moaned, clasping her head between her hands. Thankfully the world, and her stomach, began to settle again.

She was in a dark alley, lying across a packing crate. Her leather coat was unbuttoned and open, and her clothes were gone. She sat up much more slowly than before, carefully testing the effects of being upright, and drew the coat closed against the chill. Trembling, she swayed on the crate for a long minute before slipping off, gripping the side to steady herself, and then looking about.

There was no sign of her skirt, but her blouse, or the remnants of it, were scattered around in several pieces. She hissed as she closed her legs, gasping for breath at the sudden pain and shifting her feet apart again, then walking, slowly and carefully along the alley towards the distant light.

She reached the road, and her car, parked neatly next to the sidewalk. She had no idea where she was and stumbled across to the vehicle, hoping it was open. It wasn't, but her keys were in the pocket of her coat, and a moment later she was inside the car with the heater blowing.

She ached, and her breasts felt tender. And her throat was sore, as if she had a terrible cold.

The car's clock told her it was nearly midnight. The last thing she remembered was... she had been going to visit someone, but who?

She put the car into gear and pulled away, her mind

becoming clearer with each passing minute, clouded only with exhaustion and pain now as she gazed at the street signs and tried to find her way. She gradually began to pinpoint her whereabouts, knew which way to head, and turned south.

What had happened to her prior to coming too on the old crate?

Her foot pressed down more sharply on the accelerator and the car surged forward. She felt sick. Her stomach churned. She had no strength in her limbs.

The tires screeched as she pulled into the garage of her apartment block, and she stumbled out of her car and across to the elevator.

The apartment felt comforting as she locked the door behind her, and a bit of the tension she hadn't been aware was gripping her receded. She headed straight for the bathroom, stripping off her coat as she flicked on the light – and stared in shock.

Her hair was bedraggled, matted by something sticky, and some viscous substance had dried on the underside of her chin and her throat. She wiped at it with her hands, disgusted, appalled as she smeared it off.

It was also on her breasts and in her cleavage, she discovered, and the more she looked the more she found, on her belly, and most sickening of all coating her naked sex lips and inner thighs.

And there were neat bite marks all over her, on her breasts and tummy, her hips and throat and shoulders and thighs.

She swayed on her feet, and then sank to her knees, but not before noting how mournfully pale she looked. She turned, moaning, and crawled into the shower cubicle, then reached up and turned on the water, letting it pour down over her. It was all she could do to sink back against the wall tiles for several long minutes and let the exquisitely hot water cleanse her battered body. Then she worked up the energy and some degree of enthusiasm to reach for the soap, and began to lather herself all over.

Who were they, she wondered dazedly, and how many of them had fucked her?

She lathered herself and rinsed off, then again and again before, exhausted, she dried herself, made her way from the bathroom, and fell asleep on the comforting warmth of the rug in her living room.

A shadowy face, a smile.

Flash.

Arousal. Heady, exciting.

Flash.

Darkness. Surging shadows closing in all around her.

Flash.

Intense need and lust and frantic tearing of clothing.

Flash.

Hands clawing at her body, her mouth, her throat, her breasts.

Flash.

Savage pounding inside her, hands all over her, leering faces surrounding her, blotting out the moon.

Flash.

Her body writhing in unison with the frenzied thrusting of rigid cocks. Her mouth stretched wide around a demanding erection, her throat penetrated, her legs held apart, something behind her, her anus stretched around an intruder. Her body twisted, turned, lifted. Sneering faces.

Flash.

Ecstasy. Screaming wails of ecstasy. Hers.

Chapter Eight

She woke up with the sun on her face, looking out the glass balcony door. She felt instantly alert and sat up, frowning. As she rose to her feet she remembered taking a shower, but nothing after that. But she did feel clean and pure, strong and filled with energy.

Her hair looked healthy, shining lustrously. There were no bite marks on her body, and no bruises. Tentatively she touched a finger against her sex and felt a little burst of excitement, but no pain.

Had it all been a dream? Had it all been a horrible nightmare?

It was Monday morning. Had she any reason or excuse not to go in to work? There was nothing desperately needing her attention there, and she had worked on her Sunday off. There were the missing girls of course, but she was fairly peripheral in the case, else she'd not have had the weekend off, and she really didn't feel like going to work today. She would either be driving from place to place carrying out routine inquiries, which for the most part amounted to nothing more than interview sheets to go on the pile, or she'd be stuck somewhere doing research, checking records of sex offenders or investigating people who had access to computerized information on the girls.

It was boring, boring, boring. Of course she'd only been a detective for a few months and she knew it would get better eventually, after she'd put in some time. She would be trusted more, be given more important assignments, but in the meantime it was all pretty dull.

And she felt hyper, like running and jumping, like going wild. There was an energy in her which made it hard to sit still for long. Of course if she wound up partnered with Sara again things could get quite energetic, but that was dangerous because someone might find out.

She could make work more interesting without running a major risk, though. She felt a flare of heat and a tightening in her chest at the thought, and padded across the bedroom to her dresser, pulling it open, feeling a slightly breathless sensation as she gazed down inside. She had bought more than dresses on her Friday shopping expedition.

There was what appeared, at first glance, to be a collection of thin leather straps sitting in the drawer. As she lifted them up they spread out, attached by metal rings. One strap dropped heavily, weighted down by two fat leather tubes. Both were attached to the strap by a quarter inch metal bolt. One was a stubby butt plug, the other a stout dildo. Both were softly padded and encased in leather, and the thought of wearing them to work began to make her hands shake with excitement. No one would know. No one would guess. It would be a secret, like the rings she found herself constantly toying with. It was insane of course, but...

Leah bent over slightly, gripping the butt plug, twisting it softly from side to side as she pushed it in and out, forcing it deeper and deeper with each push, gasping, bending further over as the plug forced her little opening to relax and accept the foreign object.

'Oh!' she squealed as it slid into her rectum. She pushed it further and her anus closed behind it, with only the tiny bolt sliding inside her.

She pressed the dildo against her sex lips, not the least

surprised to find she was already wet. She was always wet these days. She groaned in pleasure as it slid into her, twisting it in her fingers, rolling her hips a little as it passed over her clitoris. She pushed it in fully, gasping a little as it filled her, but though it was fat and long it was soft and pliable and very snug.

She pulled the rest of the straps up over her shoulders. They were little wider than her thumbs, encircled her breasts, and fitted tightly around her waist. The leather was soft but firm against her flesh, the metal rings cold at first but warming as they followed the contours of her body.

The final strap, the one with the dildo and butt plug attached, was drawn down between her buttocks and thighs. She squealed a little as she pulled the strap up at the front to buckle it to the ring at the centre of her stomach, gasping as the strap dug between the lips of her sex and forced the dildo deeper still.

Pulling on the ingenious harness tightened it entirely, and the straps that encircled her breasts pulled in more sharply, squeezing the soft flesh into taut globes. Then she turned, breathing deeply, gazing dreamily at her reflection in the mirror.

She picked up her brush and worked it through her hair, then stepped back, straightening her shoulders. That caused the straps to dig in even more severely and she let out an involuntary groan. Her nipples, she noted, stroking them softly with her fingertips, were even more erect than was usual now. The lower strap cut between the bare lips of her sex, squeezing deliciously and painfully against the ring impaling her clitoris.

She looked at her reflection, eyes sparkling, then turned slightly and looked again over her shoulder. Smiling, she put on a black silk blouse and a pair of black trousers, quite businesslike, especially beneath a black blazer, then she chose her shoes, not stilettos but fairly high-heeled, and slipped her feet into them.

Perhaps Mbweni might not approve, but she didn't much care what the woman thought just then.

She walked slowly back and forth, feeling the dildo and the butt plug coaxing her simmering excitement, enjoying the comforting feel of the harness embracing her, and wondered if she'd be able to get through the day without going mad with arousal.

She pulled on her leather coat and headed for the door, delighting in the wickedness she felt as she passed others on the landing and nodded politely in the elevator.

'Ah, detective, the captain wants to see you straight away,' the desk sergeant called as Leah entered the station.

Leah halted in surprise. 'Did she say what she wants?'

'Ha! The captain rarely takes me into her confidence,' he said with a snort.

She nodded and continued on, wondering what Mbweni wanted now; reasonably confident it wasn't to make her life more pleasant. Or was it? She felt a dawning sense of wary alarm, remembering Mbweni's phone call. She despised the arrogant bitch, yet in her present condition the thought of submitting to her sexually made her body tense with sexual desire.

She made her way up the stairs and then to the rear of the station where the district's higher ranking leadership had their offices, taking a deep breath as she knocked on Mbweni's door.

'Come,' she heard her superior's arrogant voice, and opened the door and entered the office, her tummy turning a little with uncertainty.

'You wanted to see me, ma'am?' she said.

'Close the door,' came the abrupt response, and Leah kept her expression neutral as she did so, then walked up to Mbweni's desk and stood before it. Mbweni was looking over report forms, and showed no particular urgency to deal with her. Leah was determined not to show any indiscipline, and waited patiently until the woman got around to telling her why she was wasting her time, and after several long minutes Mbweni closed the file she was studying and looked up, her demeanor one of confident arrogance.

'Detective MacInnes,' she said, 'I expect you are aware of police regulations dealing with the standards of professional behavior?'

Leah blinked in confusion. 'Yes, ma'am,' she said.

Mbweni nodded. 'And tell me, how do you believe the regulations would interpret the actions of a police officer who, whilst on duty, decided to spend all morning engaging in a sexual interlude with a colleague?'

Leah stared, and with a shock realized Mbweni somehow knew about Friday morning with Sara Yi. She felt the blood drain from her face, and struggled to keep her expression from betraying the shock she was feeling. 'I... I doubt they would approve,' she said, struggling to keep her voice steady. Mbweni would have no proof, she told herself, her mind racing, and even if Sara confessed it would be her word against Leah's.

'So you do understand that, officer?'

'Yes, ma'am,' Leah said.

'And yet you decided to indulge yourself regardless.'

'I don't know what you mean, ma'am,' she said, standing stiffly.

Mbweni raised an eyebrow, then pushed her chair back and turned to the credenza behind her. She pressed a button on a VCR sitting on a lower shelf and the television monitor

124

came to life. As Leah stared at the screen her eyes widened, and she felt as if she'd been punched in the gut. She saw herself slumped back on the sofa naked, legs spread wide, knees drawn back, as Yi lapped at her pussy. She blushed furiously as the scene changed to her fucking the Asian girl with the large dildo. 'Stop it!' she pleaded in a strangled voice, knowing it was hopeless when she saw the date and time clearly showing in the bottom right corner of the screen. 'Please, ma'am, I don't need to see anymore.'

Mbweni flicked the recording off and turned to confront her. 'So you don't know what I mean?'

'H-how did you get that?' she stuttered.

'That is not important.'

'But it's a violation of my privacy,' Leah complained.

'It was submitted to me anonymously by a concerned citizen,' Mbweni said. 'And I would be negligent in my duty if I did not confront you with it.'

'Are you kidding me?' Leah gasped. 'How did anyone manage to film that?'

'I'm sure you would know that better than I, MacInnes. However, my concern is not with your sexual promiscuity or perversity but with what you do whilst on duty. Now, have you anything to say for yourself?'

Leah took a deep breath in an effort to calm herself. 'How did anyone manage to film us?' she demanded again.

'My only concern lies in what to do with you,' Mbweni stated, easily deflecting the question. 'Clearly I cannot overlook this, but if I draw up formal charges against you involving such prurient material the media will certainly become involved. It's the kind of scandal the press adores.'

Leah hated the woman, but there was no question she was right. The press would lap up such a salacious scoop and it would destroy her career.

'But on the other hand,' Mbweni continued, 'it is not

absolutely necessary that this sordid episode should become public, although you must certainly be punished, of course.' She smiled a cunning smile, and Leah felt outrage and then, infuriatingly, arousal.

'What do you want?' she demanded through tight lips.

Mbweni smiled and got up, moving around her desk and then behind Leah, who felt her stomach lurch as the woman locked the door and then leaned back against it.

'Let me see what you have to offer,' she suggested breezily.

'You bitch,' Leah said, but the words did not have the venom they should have, for her pussy was tingling with the growing certainty she would have to submit to the woman, and the remembrance of what she wore beneath her clothes.

'And I shall also have to punish you for that disrespectful little outburst, of course,' Mbweni said, thin eyebrows arched. 'And I must warn you, I'm an old fashioned woman who believes in corporal punishment for impertinent creatures like you.'

Leah stood motionless, returning her challenging stare. 'Come on then,' Mbweni went on, 'let's see what I'm getting.'

'Not here,' Leah said warily.

Mbweni shook her head, smiling with amusement. 'Here and now.'

'No, I...' Words failed Leah.

'Now, and at once,' Mbweni snapped.

Leah's anger flared at the arrogance of the woman, but her pussy flared as well. And then Mbweni pushed away from the door and walked slowly, sinuously, stopping inches from her. Leah stood stiffly, her heart pounding, as Mbweni's hands rose and her fingers ran up the lapels of Leah's blazer. They slipped inside, drawing the blazer back, and her dark eyes lowered.

'Mmmmm,' she purred, 'are you feeling chilly, detective?'

Leah's face flushed with indignant anger and embarrassment, then she gasped as Mbweni's hands slid onto her breasts and cupped them. At first there was smugness in Mbweni's eyes, then surprise, and then a triumphant sense of understanding as she felt the rings and leather beneath the thin blouse.

Slowly, tormentingly, her fingers moved to the blouse buttons and she began to undo them one by one. Leah reached for her wrists to halt the unwelcome progress, but they were contemptuously swatted away. Closing her eyes in resignation, Leah dropped her hands to her sides as the woman completed her objective and then pulled the blouse out of the waistband of her trousers. She heard the chuckle of delight as the woman saw what Leah wore beneath, and then gasped, opening her eyes again at the feel of fingers on her ringed and naked nipples.

'Well, well, well, so this is how the prim little southern girl dresses for a day at work,' she said in a sneering voice. She pushed her hands upward and eased the opened blouse and blazer back over Leah's shoulders, and they dropped to the floor behind Leah, who dropped her gaze, too mortified to resist or try to explain anything, and buffeted by secret waves of excitement at the touch of the woman's hands on her body.

Mbweni traced the line of the strap going down her front to her trousers, then quickly undid them and let them fall around Leah's ankles, giving a soft chuckle of appreciation as she saw the bare pubis and the strap digging up between the lips of her sex.

'You surprise me, MacInnes,' she said. 'You really do. And here I thought you were such a conservative girl. Of course, your little games with Yi should have warned me.'

Leah tried desperately to brace herself against the rippling shocks of pleasure that rolled through her body as Mbweni fondled her, pushing her back against the edge of the desk and reaching for the strap between her legs. She traced it up and down between her pussy lips, and then undid the clasp holding it around her waist. The strap dropped, but remained firmly between her pussy lips, and only when Mbweni began to pull did she realize why, and Leah felt more shame as the woman tugged and her sex lips spread apart to reveal the black dildo embedded within.

Mbweni twisted Leah around and gripped the back of her neck, forcing her to bend forward across her desk, and Leah gasped as she slapped her sharply on the bottom. She felt the woman's finger tracing the line of her sex, sliding against the moist flesh clutched tightly around the dildo, and closed her eyes as she felt the rude implement being pulled out.

'My, what a long one,' Mbweni smirked, and Leah let out a cry of shock as the woman suddenly eased it back into her, hard and deep. Her hands clawed back, her body twisting, trying to reach for the woman, only for Mbweni to grip her hair and tug her head back, Leah gripping Mbweni's wrist to try and counter the pain. Her back was arched, her legs spread, and Mbweni used her position ruthlessly, pumping the dildo in and out, each time she thrust it deep her knuckles rubbing Leah's pierced clitoris.

Leah's mind turned to jelly, her thinking processes disintegrating. Her fingers clung feebly to Mbweni's wrist, her body trembling as she gasped in dazed ecstasy. Her legs trembled and her hips began to grind against the desk edge as Mbweni thrust the dildo in and out, and as she climaxed loudly Mbweni cursed and was forced to abandon her grip on Leah's hair and clamp her hand over

128

Leah's mouth as she writhed with pleasure on the desk.

Only when Leah's body went limp did Mbweni draw her hand away from the girl's mouth and still the movement of the dildo, burying it deep within her pussy and fastened the strap back into place. 'You are clearly in the wrong line of work, MacInnes,' she said, purring with delight. 'I think I'm going to enjoy you immensely.' She bent over Leah's clothing and found her handcuffs, quickly cuffing the exhausted girl's wrists behind her back. 'Oh, we're going to have so much fun together,' she said. 'Of course, you must be punished like the naughty girl you are. We must maintain the highest standards of discipline here at all times.'

Leah sobbed as her hair was pulled again, but the handkerchief Mbweni pressed into her mouth stifled the sound abruptly, Leah's lips stretched around the makeshift gag. Mbweni tutted. 'Such a noisy girl,' she gently admonished. 'We don't want anyone to know of the fun we're having, now do we?'

Leading Leah by the hair, she walked the shaken young woman to her chair behind the desk, then sat down and guided her lovely plaything across her lap. Leah moaned feebly but to no avail as she was positioned just as the woman wanted her.

'Such a pretty bottom,' Mbweni cooed, stroking the softly rounded curves of Leah's upraised buttocks. She opened a drawer and drew out a pair of leather gloves, then drew one over her right hand and leather-covered fingers stroked the strap digging into Leah's sex. Mbweni chuckled, then lifted her hand and slapped it hard across the lovely naked bottom before her. Leah yelped, her legs kicking weakly as the stinging impact made her eyes widen.

'Such a naughty, naughty girl,' Mbweni mocked.

The gloved hand caressed the blotchy pinkness spreading across the twin globes for a few quiet seconds, then Leah yelped as her boss spanked her again, then again, then again, with three sharp strikes that made her body shudder.

'But don't you worry, MacInnes,' Mbweni said, 'I shall be your mentor in this as in many things.'

Another sharp spank made her bottom flare with heat, and the woman began to punish her rhythmically with steady blows that made her bottom throb with fiery pain, tears of outrage and shame filling her eyes, but when she felt the woman's fingers move down to her sex and rub her sense of injustice dissolved under a flood of pleasure as another climax gripped her.

Leah lay on the floor, panting for breath as Mbweni looked smugly down at her.

'Did we enjoy our little spanking, MacInnes?' the woman goaded. 'It certainly appeared so.' She reached down and gripped Leah's hair, hauling her dazed victim to her knees. She was wearing a skirt, which she drew slowly up, revealing her long legs and no underwear, and abruptly pulled the panting girl's face against her sex and tugged the handkerchief from her mouth.

'Show me how respectful you can be, MacInnes,' she ordered. 'Convince me why I shouldn't leak that video tape to parties who would find it very interesting.'

Leah tried stubbornly to twist away but Mbweni easily held her face between her thighs. She was shaven like Leah, and as Leah's lips nestled against the woman's sex lips she shuddered with a secret thrill. She winced as the woman twisted her fist in her hair, then obediently pushed her tongue out and licked a wet trail over the woman's labia.

'That's it,' Mbweni sighed. 'That's very nice, you

naughty girl.'

Leah could taste her, and pushed her tongue deeper, slipping it between the lips and lapping up and down between them. The floor was hard against her knees and her wrists twisted futilely in the handcuffs as she licked with growing intensity the woman's sex. She felt degraded, shamed, humiliated, and incredibly aroused because of it. Her tongue searched out Mbweni's clitoris and found it, and the woman's hips rocked forward, squeezing her face into her groin as she responded.

'Ooh, you naughty girl,' she groaned. 'You clever, naughty girl…'

Chapter Nine

'Where are we going?' Leah asked.

'Where are we going, ma'am,' Mbweni corrected her.

'Where are we going, ma'am?' Leah asked again, obediently.

'You shouldn't question your superiors, MacInnes. If I want you to know something I'll tell you.'

Leah bit her tongue.

'The correct response, MacInnes, is *yes ma'am.*'

'Yes, ma'am.'

They were in Mbweni's car, which was at least a relief from being in Mbweni's office. The combination of shame, anger and excitement had left an indelible impression upon her. Mbweni had demonstrated so effortlessly that she was Leah's absolute mistress by spanking her and then taunting her while she made her perform oral sex on her. Infuriatingly she still found herself terribly aroused by Mbweni, and some submissive part of her waited keenly for the woman to make further use of her.

'I must say I am quite surprised at you, MacInnes,' the woman said. 'I know what a slut Yi is, of course, at how easy it would be to turn her into a doting little sex toy, but I thought you would be a much greater challenge.' Her hand dropped from the steering wheel onto Leah's thigh, and Leah stiffened as it began to stroke up and down. 'But it is not always easy to judge a person,' Mbweni went on, sliding her fingers onto Leah's lap and squeezing her pussy through her trousers, 'and it means I can use you in ways other than the obvious, much sooner than I had anticipated.'

'I thought you had already used me entirely to your satisfaction,' Leah said tightly, looking out the window, and heard contempt and amusement in Mbweni's reply.

'Oh, I shall use you much more thoroughly than that, young lady. But I had another type of use in mind, as we shall see shortly, the same type of use to which I've put Sara Yi.'

Leah turned her head to look at the woman driving. 'What does that mean?' she asked.

Instead of answering Mbweni smiled coldly and pulled into a small car park, where she turned off the engine, then opened the door and got out. After a moment's hesitation Leah did the same, wrapping her jacket more tightly around herself as she gazed around. They were in a run down area but she had no idea where, nor did she think Mbweni would welcome questions as the woman moved towards a steel door in a brick wall. She followed as Mbweni opened the unlocked door, and then followed her into a dimly lit corridor. The yellowed linoleum floors were old and peeling, and there were cracks in the stone walls as they went down several steps and continued deeper into the building. In the distance Leah could hear music and the hubbub of voices.

They turned into a room lit by red light. It was a bar, a dingy dive of a bar with a scattering of round wooden tables focused on small stage set against the far wall. The only real lights in the room were over the bar, and over the stage, and a girl was gyrating naked on the stage, swinging unsteadily around a metal pole. Leah thought it was a seedy little place, but her stomach fluttered excitedly as she stared over at the stripper, remembering what Mbweni had told her on the phone, and recalling her own lurid fantasies.

This was not a place where sophisticated men in suits watched beautiful women dance tastefully and shed their clothes with artistry and erotic precision. The girl on the stage looked neither talented nor particularly beautiful, even under the dim lighting, and the men sitting around were grungy and poorly dressed, drinking beer from plastic tumblers, depriving drunks of the convenient use of glasses or bottles for weapons.

Leah felt dirty even being in such a place, and squirmed a little as every male eye which noticed them turned their way, dark and hungry. She felt like a lamb that had wandered into a wolf den.

But Mbweni did not seem uncomfortable in the place, and led her to a free table near the stage, sitting down easily. Leah gazed with distaste at the plastic chair, wishing she could have it washed before sitting on it, then sat gingerly, keeping her hands and arms away from the sticky, stained top of the cheap table.

One of the men sniggered drunkenly and threw a coin at the girl on stage, who caught it neatly. There would be no ten dollar notes slipped into G-strings here, Leah thought in disgust.

Another man threw his half empty cup of beer and the liquid spattered across the girl's breasts and belly as others laughed in drunken amusement. But the dancer ignored it, turning and twisting, her eyes even more glassy than those of her drunken audience, her movements rarely coinciding with the music pounding from a nearby speaker.

A waitress in yellow shorts and a tight boob tube moved towards them but was stopped by a man at another table grabbing her wrist and yanking her aside. He demanded three more beers for him and his mates, as his hand roughly kneaded the girl's bottom through the shorts, which were so brief the lower slopes of her buttocks were exposed. She made no complaint, but merely nodded wearily before continuing on to them.

'What you want?' she asked.

'Two vodkas,' Mbweni ordered, handing the girl a bill, who nodded and headed back to the bar.

'What are we doing here, ma'am?' Leah asked nervously.

'Don't you ever want to get out and about, MacInnes?' Mbweni asked. 'All work and no play, as they say.'

'This is not my idea of entertainment,' Leah said.

'Show us your cunt!' a man to their right roared, laughter following the crude demand, and the girl turned her bottom his way, bending over and wagging it at him as he laughed along with the rest. Leah grimaced with disgust as the girl thrust two fingers into her sex and pulled it open wide, revealing the gleaming pink interior. Someone threw beer at her and it splashed across her back and bottom, dribbling down her thighs as she slowly straightened and turned again.

'Do you think you'd like to be up there, MacInnes?' Mbweni asked.

'No,' Leah answered adamantly, 'I certainly wouldn't.'

The girl lay on her back, legs straight up in the air, and then let her feet slowly part. She lowered them to the floor and raised her pelvis, rolling her hips as she pumped her fingers inside her sex.

After a while her stint was over and she left the small stage, another girl taking her place. She was no more talented than the first, though with larger breasts which seemed to fascinate the drooling audience. Their vodkas arrived, but Leah wrinkled her nose at the plastic cup, not wanting any part of touching, much less drinking anything from the dirty little bar.

135

'I bet this place hasn't seen a health inspector in years,' she said.

'Not ever, I'd say,' Mbweni agreed, sipping her drink. 'It's not a licensed establishment.'

The first girl was in the audience now, wearing a tiny slip dress, moving amongst the men searching for those willing to purchase a private dance. One nearby agreed, and she began to grind against him as his mates laughed and cheered him on. The girl was soon naked, straddling his lap as she slid her breasts up and down against his face.

'Why are we here?' Leah asked.

'A lot of drugs move through this place,' Mbweni said. 'An enormous amount of drugs.'

'I don't see anything.'

'That's because it's all done in the toilets, behind the bar, and they're wary whenever strangers show up. They know their clientele very well here.'

A third girl stepped out on stage, and it was almost an anticlimax but still jarring when Leah realized it was Sara Yi. The girl did not look as dazed as the others, but her eyes were haunted as she stepped through the curtain and moved uncertainly forward.

'What is she doing here?' Leah hissed under her breath.

'She volunteered to work here undercover, as it were,' Mbweni replied in a low, amused voice.

Sara was wearing a sexy pleated skirt and a blouse, and she cringed visibly as men called out obscene remarks and racist insults. She began to dance awkwardly to the music, her hips swaying from side to side, and then her fingers rose, slowly undoing the buttons of her blouse.

'Why are you making her do this?' Leah demanded.

'I didn't *make* her do anything,' Mbweni insisted. 'It was her choice. Besides, watch her. She really gets quite into it.'

'But I don't—'

'I said watch.'

Sara looked desperately embarrassed as she pulled her blouse from the waistband of her skirt and slowly drew it open, revealing a lacy black bra, then squealed and stumbled back against the pole as half the contents of a cup of beer splattered against her face and chest, then turned her back to them, rolling her hips as she peeled the beer-stained blouse off her shoulders and dropped it to the grimy stage. She turned again and again, her fingers fumbling at the catch of her skirt, trying to undo it.

'Show us your tits, you fucking chink!' someone bellowed drunkenly.

'Suckee suckee for fifty cents!' another roared, clearly reveling in the laughter his unfunny comment produced from his fellow drinkers.

'Get your clothes off, bitch!' shouted another.

The skirt slid own Sara's legs and she kicked it off, almost tripping as she did so.

'She dances like a horse,' Mbweni said, shaking her head. 'I'm sure you'd be much more graceful.'

Sara danced awkwardly in stiletto heels and her flimsy underwear, then undid her bra and slid it off. There was a look to her face now, and as she kicked off her shoes she began to move more lithely, her eyes darting about at the front row of the audience. Her hips rolled and her hands moved up and down her undulating body as scattered cheers goaded her on.

Then her fingers peeled her thong down and off and, naked, she danced with more fluency. More beer was flung at her, but now she seemed to bask in it, arching her back, cupping her breasts, then turning and grasping the pole to her slick body and twisting around it.

'Pink! Pink! Pink!' the audience yelled.

She twisted and twirled, then dropped to her knees, crawling along on all fours, rolling her bottom lewdly, a smoldering look in her eyes. She turned her bottom to them, spreading her legs, pushing her sex out. Her fingers slid beneath her and up into her pussy, pumping in and out as more beer showered onto her. She rolled onto her back, knees spread wide, bottom rising and falling as her hands moved over her wet body, stroking and fondling, then down between her thighs. Leah blushed as she saw three fingers thrusting in and out of Sara's pussy, watching her knees draw far back, spreading wide as she pretended – if it was pretense – to masturbate.

She climbed up the pole, dragging herself up, keeping her legs spread wide, her bottom out. More beer was heaved across the stage, plastering her hair, her entire body glistening as she curled her legs around the pole and rode up and down against it.

'Don't worry,' Mbweni said. 'She'll get her reward in a little room backstage. For twenty dollars she'll suck any of these men off. For fifty they can choose whether to fuck her in the cunt or in the ass.' To Leah the blatantly crude language didn't seem right coming from the lips of her boss. 'So she's pulling in quite a useful addition to her normal salary.'

Leah had heard enough. She rose and headed for the door, slapping aside a filthy hand that reached out to grope her bottom as she passed. She breathed deeply once out in the car park, but felt dirty, as though she needed a shower.

Mbweni took her time following and smiled when she saw Leah's glare. 'Have I offended your precious sense of morality, young lady?' she mocked.

'You threatened to fire her if she didn't do this, didn't

you?' Leah challenged.

'I have no power to fire anyone, MacInnes, you know that,' Mbweni said casually. 'All I have the power to do is recommend someone be investigated by Internal Affairs. If Yi is so ashamed of her conduct she prefers this to having it dragged into the light, well, that's her choice.'

'And is that what you have in mind for me?' Leah demanded.

Mbweni smiled. 'Not quite, no. You're far too middle class for such a place, and frankly, far too beautiful. A woman of color like Yi can get away with it. She can pretend her English is much worse than it is, pretend she's a helpless, illegal immigrant. But no one would believe someone like you would work in a place like that.'

She got into the car and Leah reluctantly slid in beside her. 'So I suppose you've got me earmarked of a more upscale strip club,' she said sarcastically.

'No, my dear, you're going to an upscale escort agency,' Mbweni announced as she pulled out of the car park and turned into the road.

'Excuse me?' Leah gasped.

'You heard me. We can provide you with a suitable background, and you'll have no difficulty proving your credentials.' She smiled wolfishly. 'And then you can start gathering evidence as you go on appointments. The agency in question is owned by organized crime. We want you to get their records for us, particularly client names, and more importantly we want to see where the money is going.'

'I won't do it,' Leah insisted.

'You won't fuck a few wealthy men?' Mbweni taunted. 'Of course you will, and in return I won't leak that little old video I have in my possession.'

'I won't do it,' Leah said again.

'Oh, I think you will,' Mbweni said confidently. 'Just think of what such devotion to duty will do for your career... and think of how humiliated you'll be if your little dalliance with Yi were to be common knowledge.'

'Why don't you think about what the courts will do when they find out I got my information by fucking people,' Leah countered.

'But they won't find out, dear girl. You'll never be identified as a police officer; you'll never have to testify. Provided, of course, that you recover sufficient evidence to force a plea bargain.'

'Is that what this is, a plea bargain?' Leah demanded.

Mbweni smiled. 'Of course. Your punishment is withheld in exchange for cooperation.'

Within a half hour they were pulling into the garage beneath the district police headquarters. Mbweni parked in a distant corner of the garage and turned off the engine, then turned to face Leah, sliding her skirt up as she did so.

'Now let us see if you remember what you've been taught,' she said, leaning back against the door, drawing her legs apart and revealing her naked sex. Leah nibbled her lip anxiously and looked around the empty garage, then sighing resignedly, leant forward, gasping as Mbweni seized her hair, drawing her face down between her parted thighs. Her tongue flickered out and Mbweni tugged at her hair impatiently. 'Come on, you can do better than that, slut.'

Leah slid her tongue between the woman's pussy lips, pressing her mouth hard against Mbweni's sex, and winced as she felt a hand squeezing beneath her and spitefully squeezing her breast.

'I'm sure you'll be an excellent assistant, once you're fully trained as I want you,' Mbweni sighed.

Chapter Ten

Leah downed the brandy in one gulp and then gasped, panting for breath as it burned her throat. It had been a shattering day, almost from start to finish. First had come that humiliating meeting with Mbweni, then her shocking trip to the strip bar, no doubt to be shown what Mbweni could do to her if she annoyed her sufficiently, and then an 'interview' with the manager of the *Little Sisters* escort agency.

She had at least been allowed to return home and remove the harness and dildos before going to see the man, but that had done little to revive her pride, for she'd been forced to remove her clothes soon after entering the man's office for an utterly humiliating interview. Demonstrating her value, which included how she looked naked, was horrible. Yet she'd had little choice, and her face flamed as she walked to and fro, naked, under the smirking gaze of the manager. And then came the inevitable requirement that she demonstrate her sexual skills.

Her mind shied away from even remembering that, and she thumped the empty glass down on the cabinet and tore her clothes off, flinging them on the floor and kicking them away. That bitch, Mbweni. She would pay her back somehow. She poured another drink and drank it more slowly as she prepared for a much needed shower.

His office was filthy, the door off its hinge, hanging wide open. On her knees she had to perform oral sex on him to demonstrate her commitment, her willingness, her abilities. Only the best girls for his agency, he muttered, stabbing his erection into the back of Leah's throat.

She stepped under the cascading water, turning it hotter still, trying to erase the memories of how he'd come on her face, then ordered her to bend over his desk as one of his men, a large thug, joined them and fucked her roughly from behind. Shameful it had been, but worse was that her 'acting skills' he had later praised had been entirely natural. She did not fake the orgasm that gripped her, but fought desperately against it to no avail.

She soaped and scrubbed herself, thinking of the filthy hovel where Sara danced and, if Mbweni was being honest, prostituted herself. How had they allowed themselves to fall so completely under the woman's control?

She winced a little as her fingers slid down between her legs, gasping at the thrumming pleasure and soreness she felt. Her hands slid back, around her hip, over her bottom, and she winced once again.

The bitch! For this was no ordinary escort agency. No, the clientele of *Little Sisters* had a particular penchant. So she'd been positioned over the manager's lap and soundly spanked, to see how she reacted, how she coped with the beating. For there was big money in allowing men to spank pretty girls, and that was the house specialty. But her bottom was already sore from Mbweni's earlier spanking, so she squealed and squirmed right from the start.

She rinsed and soaped again, furious, knowing Mbweni had simply chosen not to tell her, knowing how amused the woman must have been. Still, she consoled herself, she had endured it bravely. And in truth she was the main investigator into the dealings of the agency, not a nearly nameless door ringer, and if Mbweni could really give her the credit without letting out what she had been forced to do to get the information it would indeed be a feather in her cap.

It was dangerous though; for if they found out she was a cop she'd be in real trouble. But how would they? Why should they suspect such a thing?

She stepped out of the shower and dried off, then used the blow-dryer on her hair before fetching herself another glass of brandy.

The agency was raking in serious money, and quite a bit of it wound up with the girls. It was a top of the line operation, and their services went for two thousand dollars per two hour visit, and two thirds of that went to the girls. She could easily make more in a day than she made in a month in the police, and none of it taxed.

She heard the phone ring and turned, frowning. There seemed something indefinably wrong with the sound warbling softly through the quiet apartment. She looked at it, not moving, listening as it warbled again. She had no desire to speak with anyone. Her inclination was to let it ring, to let the machine pick up.

It rang again, and she found herself fighting the urge to cross the floor and pick up, an urge which grew with every insistent warble. It continued to ring and she felt a moment's confusion, wondering why the answering machine had not kicked in. Then she bit her lip lightly, irritated that whoever was ringing her continued to wait, continued to let the phone warble. But perhaps it was urgent. She glared at the phone as if it were a contest of wills between them. Would they never hang up? If she did pick up and it wasn't urgent she was going to flay whoever was on the other end of the line. Defeated, she stalked across the room and snatched up the receiver.

'Yes?' she snapped.

At first she heard nothing but a soft humming. It was

not machinelike, but distinctively alive. She started to speak, to demand whoever it was speak up, but there was something disturbing about the sound, something familiar yet just out of her reach. Tension began to build within her and she felt her chest tighten and her stomach flutter.

'*Leah…*'

Her name was barely audible, a whisper, and hardly human. It was the moan of the wind going beneath a doorway yet formed into her name.

'*Leah…*'

She tried to swallow and found her throat dry. Her name was a long, soft moan.

'*Leah…*'

Louder now, but still an inhuman moan drifting through the shadows. And then something else; a soft chuckle, just as inhuman but definably male. Leah slammed the receiver down, holding it on its cradle as if in fear it would leap up at her. She was breathing raggedly, her heart pounding, her pulse racing.

The phone rang again and she let out a small yelp of shock. Her hand was still on it, her knuckles white as she clenched the receiver. It rang again and again. She would not pick it up, but nor could she bring herself to pull her hand away.

She snatched the receiver up, holding it in front of her as though it were a dangerous snake. Yet she heard the soft humming, and then that voice again. '*Leah… Leah…*'

'Leave me alone or I'll fucking kill you!' she screamed into the mouthpiece before slamming it down again.

The curtains suddenly billowed out behind her and she whirled round with a shriek as damp wind blew in through the open balcony door. She crossed quickly to shut it as the air turned ice cold, and she shivered as it blew over her nakedness. She tugged at the door, which stuck, then took the handle in both hands and managed to slide it closed with a bang.

Despite this it was very cold in her apartment. Or perhaps it was her. She crossed her arms over her breasts. It was too cold to be undressed, and her warm robe was on the sofa where she'd left it previously.

As she walked towards it the fireplace suddenly roared to life, the flames jumping and licking out at her. She shrieked and stopped abruptly, jerking back, and then yelped as she felt her wrists pulled forward. She struggled against the unseen grip, and realized it was the gold bands themselves that were straining towards each other, and she twisted and strained against the pull to no avail as slowly but remorselessly the two bands neared each other. They snapped together suddenly, like powerful magnets, and locked tightly in place.

'Shit!' she cried, turning and twisting, her arms pulling against the bands. And then she cried out again at another startling pull, stumbling sideways and then forward, her nipple rings pulling outward by an unseen force, pulling her towards the roaring fire. She pulled helplessly against the gold bands, bands that had effectively become shackles, yet she could no more break free than resist the excruciating pull on her nipples as she was drawn towards the fireplace.

The flames died like a light being switched off, but the pull drew her closer, the rings drawn upward as they reached the wall, forcing her onto the balls of her feet, then onto her toes. She watched, trembling, gasping, as the rings seemed to merge with the wall, the metal running like liquid until it melted into the wall and nothing remained of them. And her nipples, which had been stretched outward, now seemed to have merged with the wall, only her areolas still visible.

The balcony door slid open and the curtains billowed again as icy air blew in. Staring at the wall just in front of her, Leah hardly noticed at first. But as the cold increased she began to shiver violently, goose bumps rising all over her body.

'*Leah...*' the wind moaned, and her head snapped round, staring towards the door. The lights went out, leaving the room dark and shadowy, the only light the silvery glow of the moon coming through the balcony door, the curtains billowing, causing wild shadows to dance about the room.

She tried to pull back from the wall, pulled until tears filled her eyes as her nipples burned with pain. She strained against the bands pinning her wrists together, bruising her soft flesh, her teeth chattering from the cold.

'*Leah...*' the wind moaned again.

Her feet began to tremble and her calf muscles burn from the strain of holding her up, but the pain in her nipples was unbearable if she tried to ease herself down. So she maintained the awkward position as the minutes ticked slowly by. She was frozen to the core, shivering fiercely, her breath panting in visible clouds, but then she felt another harsh pull and cried out as the ring through her clitoris tugged down and sharply back. Her bottom jerked out and she cried out again at the increased pain to her nipples. The fire suddenly exploded into life again, light and heat flaring around her so that she shrieked and stumbled backwards. Her nipples came free from the wall, yet she could see the rings still straining up and forward, could still feel the remorseless pull against her sensitive buds.

From cold to hot, the fire scorched her, the flames dancing and wildly, lapping out around the edges of the hearth as though trying to reach for her. She shrieked, trying to edge further back, but with her nipples held by some unseen force, her lower body pulled away from the fire by another, she found herself leaning forward, her bottom pushed out and raised. The ring through her clitoris began to vibrate as if attached to a fine wire being plucked again and again.

A sharp pain slashed across her outthrust bottom and she cried out in startled shock. Her head twisted violently from side to side as she tried to see what had struck her, but found only flitting shadows. Another bite of pain made her hips lurch forward, and she gasped as the flames licked at her thighs, as the sharp tug on her clitoris forced her back once again. The pull on her nipples grew stronger, and she sobbed fearfully as her body was drawn helplessly forward to where the flames licked out of the fireplace. Then she was in among them, the flames dancing across her breasts, around her abdomen and her thighs. Her flesh burned as she writhed in the midst of the flames, but without the pain she dreaded and expected.

Despite Leah's brave struggles her nipples were again drawn into the wall, but this time the pull continued and her breasts followed. The wall felt like ice-cold gelatin as her breasts sank into it. Her head was drawn back desperately as her hands twisted frantically against the gold bands, but as her breasts molded into the wall her head was drawn helplessly in as well, and her world disappeared.

Her body was drawn forward and down, the inexorable pull against her nipples bending her over. She could not breath, but did not seem to need to. Her torso moved through what felt like liquid glass, which slurped sluggishly aside and around her trembling body as she continued to bend. She could see through it, after a fashion, but not far and, turning her head to look back saw nothing beyond her waist.

147

Her bottom was thrust out into the warmth of her room, her legs well apart, the pull of the gold bands around her ankles almost anchoring them to the floor. She turned her eyes back, staring ahead into a cloudy white liquid world of utter silence. Her head turned slowly in the gelatinous liquid, but there was nothing to see up, down, or from side to side.

The pull on her nipples stopped but held her in place, and then the liquid seemed to swirl around her, rolling softly, caressing her body intimately, seeping around her aching nipples.

She could still feel the flickering flames around her sex, the fire dancing around her legs and hips. And then another harsh slash of pain across her buttocks made her cry out soundlessly in the slick, oozing liquid wall that enveloped her.

Then Leah felt a scalding finger of flame touching her sex and she shuddered as it set fire to her own helpless lusts. She felt the sexual pressure rising within her, flooding into her bewildered and frightened mind.

Another lash of pain made her jerk and moan noiselessly. Then she felt a touch on her buttocks, lowering to the tops of her thighs, an almost imperceptible touch which nevertheless pressed the swollen lips of her pussy back to expose her sex to the crackling flames. She felt her sex lips spread wider, feeling her pussy opening, feeling something entering her. It was not solid, but something indefinable, neither gas nor liquid, but hot. She felt it pushing into her sex, could feel herself stretched wide, could feel whatever it was thrusting deeper inside her.

Another lash of pain cut across her bottom and she screamed soundlessly as the thing inside her began to move more rapidly, and she felt herself swamped by the sensory overload as her body pulsed with raw, carnal need.

The liquid wall flowed around her body, caressing and squeezing her breasts, swirling through her hair and over her face, her torso shuddering continuously to the aggressive thrusting against her punished buttocks. Ice burned into her upper body as fire burned at her lower, and inside her was a deep, absurdly thick something thrusting and thrusting, driving her mad with the pressure and intensity of the sexual heat roaring within her.

She could feel the thing pressing ever deeper, every thrust forcing the intruder impossibly deep into her abdomen, driving like an invisible stake through her quivering flesh. Her head rolled up and down as if floating, her mouth wide in a soundless scream, eyes narrow slits until they snapped wide, staring wildly. Her throat tightened and she gagged weakly, trying to cough without the breath to do so.

Something oozed up her throat, up into her mouth, pressing down her tongue, filling her mouth and then pushing out between her lips. It was the same sort of glassy liquid which surrounded her, but dark. It thrust out for only a moment before retreating, then thrust out again, further, and Leah knew it was the tip of the cock thrusting into her from behind.

Her jaws ached as they were forced wider and wider. The thing thickened, pumping back and forth as her eyes stared uncomprehendingly at the bloated head emerging from her mouth.

And it was consuming her. Back and forth it pumped, one immensely long cock spearing her through from end to end. The sensory storm was too much for her brain to contain. Her desperate thoughts splintered like shattered glass. She was no longer a person, merely a shell responding to the physical impulses tearing through it, and she orgasmed again and again around the black, glassy intruder thrusting out through her gaping lips.

Chapter Eleven

There was no point in fighting any longer. Leah's will had been sapped, drained away. She wasn't even sure she wanted to fight anymore.

She was trembling as she dressed, feeling distracted, fairly oblivious to what she was putting on, then slipping her feet into neat shoes and not even remembering to lock up as she left her apartment. Her mind was empty as she drove to Morales' house, but her stomach began to churn nervously as she got closer. By the time she pulled to the curb outside his foreboding place her chest was tight and she felt nauseous.

She braced herself as she stared up at the house. It looked sinister in the shadows cast by the tall trees around it. Was Morales in, waiting for her? Or had she simply gone mad?

She got out of the car and approached the front door with a feeling of dread conflicting with anxious anticipation. She needed to find out what was happening to her, what Morales was up to. What was happening to her was virtually impossible to comprehend, so she had to try and find out what tricks Morales was playing on her, and why.

The door swung open with an ominously chilling creak, and summoning her resolve she stepped in onto the polished wooden floor of the darkened home. She started forward, and then stopped, frozen to the spot. Her mind seemed to remain alert but her body went to sleep, and she stood still for long seconds. Then her hands moved up, without her will, and began to unfasten her jacket. It was a bizarre sensation. She could not feel her arms or hands. It was as if someone else were working them, making them move. She tried to stop their activity, to influence their movements in some slight way, but failed utterly. Her fingers moved decisively and confidently, tossing aside her jacket and then her blouse, undoing the clasp of her jeans and easing them down her legs. Her feet lifted one by one without her wanting them to, pulling out of the jeans and kicking her shoes off.

When she was completely nude she walked slowly deeper into the house, her instincts to turn and flee a helpless passenger within her body. Her eyes turned neither left nor right, focused straight ahead. She walked along the hall into enveloping darkness, her body continuing without hesitation, turning right, then left, then opening a small door to reveal a shadowy stairwell.

She descended into a dusty basement filled with pipes and wires, moving smoothly through it to another door, another staircase, and down it into another shadowy yet surprisingly opulent corridor. She continued along that one, admiring the rich mahogany panels that lined its walls and the colorful Persian rug along its floor. The rug was plush and deep, but the silence around her was deeper still.

Leah felt her chest growing tight with anxiety. At the end of the corridor she turned into a large room, its walls lined with enormous purple and black velvet curtains. Soft, muted light filled the room, which had comfortable furniture, oversized leather sofas and padded chairs, teak and oak tables and chests. Still the silence was oppressive. Leah crept along the curtain, her hands rising, searching for a parting and pushing them aside.

Intense fear gripped her as she peered through the parting and saw not Morales, but another man, fairly similar in looks, powerfully built and naked. With him was one of the bald girls, standing with her arms raised, bound by shackles to a pair of heavy stone pillars. The man stood behind her, his groin moving slowly and rhythmically against her bottom, and Leah caught brief glimpses of his stout erection as he thrust it into the girl, fucking her ass.

The girl's head rolled slowly as it lay back against his shoulder, and she watched, eyes wide, as his lips parted and Leah saw his sharp canines, and she inhaled sharply in awe as his mouth widened and came down against the girl's throat and he bit into the soft, vulnerable flesh. The girl jerked slightly but showed no other reaction, her body still rolling in time to his steady thrusts into her anus. His hands were gripping the front of her thighs, holding her legs apart as he thrust into her. His lips remained locked against her throat as her eyes grew glassy, and he swallowed repeatedly.

His hips moved faster, his groin slapping repeatedly against her buttocks as he increased his stroke. Leah heard a low growl as he gave a final deep thrust and stopped moving, buried deep within the girl's body. He seemed to collapse a little, his fingers loosening their hold on her thighs, and slowly his mouth rose from her and two dark drops trickled down her pale throat as her body went limp.

Leah backed away, filled with fear, her body still being controlled somehow, as if manipulated by some unholy puppeteer. She allowed the curtain to fall together again and continued along into a smaller room, a fireplace giving off a comforting yellow light as the flames crackled gently. Another of the shaven girls was there, kneeling back on her heels, knees spread wide, arms behind her back, and Leah could see she was impaled on a thick metal pipe of some sort, the naked lips of her sex stretched wide around it. A small chain was attached to her clitoral ring and locked to the base of the column thrust into her.

Leah moved forward slowly and stopped before her. The girl made no sound. Her large blue eyes watched Leah approach with no sign of emotion. Leah circled her and noted that her wristbands were locked together behind her back.

'Hello,' Leah whispered, mildly startled at her ability to speak. The girl looked at her without expression. 'I... I'm looking for Morales.' The girl might as well have been stone but for the rise and fall of her breasts as she breathed.

'You've found him.'

Leah shrieked and whirled around to see the man standing right behind her. She should have tried to flee, her mind was screaming at her to do so, but there was something about his eyes, something deep and fathomless, that held her unable to move.

'Good evening, my dear,' he continued. 'I'm pleased you have come to me at last.'

Leah stared at him in wonder. He was so handsome. Much more so than she remembered. He might have been the most astonishingly attractive man she had ever seen in her life, and she felt her tummy flip at the sight of his beauty.

He took a step forward and again she felt a surge of fear, yet it melted away in an instant and she dropped slowly to her knees before him. He was not merely an impossibly beautiful man; she also felt a sense of awe grip her. His hand lifted and gently stroked her hair and she felt like swooning, then grasped his hand and pressed his knuckles against her cheek, against her lips, love shining in her eyes as she licked gently at his warm skin.

'Welcome again to my home,' he said, his voice softly melodious, drifting around her like gentle music.

She tried to speak, but could not make her mouth work. She was on the verge of tears, overwhelmed by her trepidation and lust. 'Master,' she finally managed.

His lips curled into a knowing smile. 'Indeed,' he said.

Two of the girls were suddenly beside her, gripping her arms, lifting her to her feet as he turned away. Leah felt bereft for a moment to see him go, and needed no urging to hurry after, the girls helping to support her as they followed him across the room. He sat in a large chair and the girls stepped back, letting Leah again sink slowly to her knees before him.

'Master,' she felt compelled to whisper again, her voice shaking with devotion. Her trembling hands reached out to grasp his ankle, desperate to show him the adoration she felt. She leaned lower and licked his shoe and moaned, pressing her cheek against the lustrous polished leather, touching her lips to his ankle and shin.

'Master,' she whispered again, her mind swirling dizzily, a fog clouding her thoughts. She kissed her way up his leg, fingers reaching uninvited for his groin and trembling, unfastened them, drawing down his zipper, reaching in and, with a sense of rapture, folding around his semi-flaccid penis.

Leah drew him out, staring wide-eyed, lust and elation filling her thoughts as she rocked forward and gently licked the head. Her lips parted slightly and she kissed it, moaning contentedly as she lowered her head, taking him deeper, filling her mouth with him.

She felt his fingers stroking her hair and shuddered with an inexplicable but intense desire to please him, working her lips up and down his erection as it stiffened and thickened. Her jaw was forced wider and she gloried in his strength and power, forcing herself deeper and deeper onto it. She remembered vaguely through the drifting fog that she had taken him into her throat some other time before.

She gurgled weakly as the bloated head pushed into her throat, forcing herself slowly down the long length of his shaft. Devotion and longing overwhelmed her as she tightened her lips around the base of his cock, nestling her nose in his wiry pubic hair.

Why was she doing this?

It was a foolish question, easily dismissed, for at that moment he was everything to her.

Leah moaned around his cock and drew her lips slowly back up, rising until the smooth head was lodged just between her stretched lips. Her hands moved, massaging his testicles as she licked him, as he gazed affectionately down at her.

'Now, little one,' he said gently, and she knew what he wanted.

As though in a dream Leah turned, positioning herself on all fours, spreading her knees and raising her bottom. She panted breathlessly as she waited, tense with need as she looked over her shoulder and watched him getting down behind her.

She felt the pressure against her sex and groaned in elation as she felt the fat head sinking into her. It was glorious to feel him inside her, to feel herself so stretched and so full.

His powerful hands gripped her hips and she felt her heart pound with delight at every new touch of him. With a stab of his hips he thrust hard and deep and her head jerked up as she cried out in pleasure and pain.

He thrust again, and again she cried out as he drove his stiff cock deep within her clutching sheath. It was uncomfortable but that didn't matter at all. The pleasure was feverish, and she could barely hold herself still as he began to fuck her, and only did so because she somehow knew he wanted her to.

Morales knew what he was doing, knew how to use her thoroughly. His fingers played music on her body as his cock moved with increasing velocity, driving into her. He pulled free repeatedly, leaving her empty, only to thrust in and make her tensed legs quiver with the pleasure of being penetrated so fully.

She was so close to a powerful climax, and yet she could not quite fall over the edge. She remained just below the peak, gasping and moaning as his mighty staff continued to pound into her from behind.

'Ah, a new one...'

Leah barely heard the voice. It wasn't until Morales replied that she raised her head to see a man standing watching them. It was the man she'd seen earlier, and now he was wearing a dark robe, holding a glass of wine, and smirking down at her. And something about the smirk goaded her.

'She shows great promise,' Morales said, continuing to thrust steadily, a part of her preening joyously under his approval.

'Will she be okay to train?' the man asked doubtfully.

Train? What was he talking about?

'I want her for something else,' Morales answered him, Leah wondering what they were talking about.

'You appear to be using her for the same thing,' the man said with another smirk.

'One use does not preclude another,' Morales countered, grinding his groin against her upraised bottom. 'Now if

157

you will leave us, please.'

The newcomer shrugged. 'Fine, perhaps I'll use her when you're done.'

Anger surged within Leah and the fog thinned. What was she doing here like this? Why was she...?

The steady thrusting of his cock was more than just distracting; the pleasure rolled over her in waves and it was almost impossible to keep her mind focused.

He leaned over her, his chest pressing down against her back as his lips began to move against the nape of her neck. She felt his teeth nipping lightly, and a sudden fear tore through her as she recalled the other man biting into the throat of the bound girl.

Yet she could not pull herself free, could not resist the intense pleasure tearing at her body and soul. She trembled with apprehension as she felt the sharpness of his teeth against the soft flesh of her throat. She had to get away. She had to run!

But she couldn't break free. Not now. Not yet. The pleasure was growing deliciously unbearable, the pressure certain to explode.

Leah cried out as his teeth pierced her flesh, sharp pain gripping her for an instant before being swept away. Her climax billowed, spreading, growing in power. She screamed in ecstasy, grinding back against his pumping groin. Fire flowed through her veins and the pleasure buffeted her. His teeth remained clamped to her throat and she heard his growl in her ear.

She was dazed as he lifted her into his arms then sat down, and she snuggled back against his shoulder and sighed in languorous comfort. His fingers stroked the hair back from her forehead and she opened her eyes wearily. She tried to reach for him, but discovered her wrists were behind her back, the metal bracelets locked together.

His hands moved slowly down her body, and fire followed them. 'What are you?' she groaned, her voice barely a whisper.

'Your master,' she heard him reply.

Chapter Twelve

There was no air. The house was a century old but the attic smelled of sawdust, of new cut wood. The floorboards were dark with age, the small window frames at either end rich with carved images of flowers. The glass itself was thick with dirt, and dust was liberally spread over the packing boxes, furniture and knickknacks covering the floor. The sun beat against the thin shingles overhead and the confined attic almost glowed with heat.

Leah lay on her side on the floor beneath a window, the setting sun turning her flesh bright and golden. Her eyes were narrowed, her jaw slack as her chest moved slowly, her breathing soft and shallow and tortured. Her ankles and wrists were drawn back behind her and held together by a thin chain. Her back was sharply and uncomfortably arched.

Beads of perspiration coated her body, slowly meandering across the smooth surface of her breasts and thighs. Her face glistened, her long brown hair damp against her brow and cheeks. Dark circles of moisture speckled the floor around her body, and then were erased as with a soft moan she shifted position, trying again to ease the strain on her shoulders and back.

The shackles around her wrists and ankles were a constant pressure against her limbs, squeezing heavily as their tight embrace bruised her tender flesh. The collar she now wore around her throat was broad, digging uncomfortably into the underside of her jaw. She spasmed weakly and a groan escaped from between her dry lips.

Soon, she thought. Soon.

Her nipples had gone numb, the iron clamps biting into them, crushing the sensitive flesh, squeezing cruelly so that both buds were swollen. Her left breast was squashed to the floor, and every time she shifted, however minutely, her moist flesh rubbed across the wood and a little tingle of pain made her nipple throb.

The sun crept lower and at last her face was out of the heat, and she mumbled her relief. She could not move, though, could not roll over. A chain was secured to the floor behind her, crossing over her thighs and attached to the ring piercing her clitoris.

The sun crept along her body until it eventually left her in the relief of the shade. What would he do to her next? Would he punish her further, or was this enough? Would he degrade her as badly as she degraded herself?

She shuddered as memories drifted around her head; dark, cruel, exquisitely arousing. Her pussy squeezed and her hips tensed. She felt the pull of the chain against her clitoris, rubbing against her exquisitely, a shard of pain making her eyes widen momentarily as she gasped.

The attic began to darken as the sun sank, shadows deepening and lengthening. She felt a vibration run through the floor as a door slammed somewhere in the building. Leah's heart beat faster and with a sudden sense of urgency she fought to roll over, to place herself as he had left her, with arms and legs beneath her.

She let out a whimper as the chain pulled against her sensitive flesh, as her aching shoulders felt new pressure against them. But then she was on her back, awkwardly positioned with her arms trapped beneath her, breasts thrust up and vulnerable as panic gripped her again.

Her eyes strained towards the stairway across the attic.

She tried to swallow, though her throat was parched. All day she had laid on the floor in the overheated attic, dead without him, as he was dead below her, several floors down in the room beneath the basement. But his touch and the unforgiving shackles were with her, reminding her of him, of his anger and the dark pleasure he forced upon her every time he touched her body.

The door below creaked and a single bare bulb flickered on overhead, throwing stark light across the attic. She heard his foot on the first step, then the second. Her pulse raced and fear and excitement twisted themselves around her insides.

Step after slow step he climbed the stairs until at last she could see him at the far end, almost appearing to rise from the floor, as from a grave. He neither smiled nor frowned to see her. His eyes were cold as he appeared to glide across the floor, carrying a shadow with him. His trousers and shirt were midnight black, his raven hair tumbling like silk around his broad shoulders.

He stood over her for a moment, brooding. Leah gazed up, panting weakly, unable to speak. He was a cruel and enigmatic man, a man of dark anger and gentle acceptance, a forgiving man who, she knew, would punish every transgression.

His black leather boots had pointed toes. One reached out and the heel pushed against her hip. She let out a soft cry as he shoved and she rolled over onto her front, and pain seared her breasts as her nipples were crushed beneath her. She rolled again instinctively, onto her side, fighting to keep silent, to not whimper like a pathetic little girl.

She watched his boot rise again, the sole coming down against her breasts. She did not, would not beg, or so she told herself, her mind spinning. He pressed down more and more heavily and the pain became severe for Leah as he gradually leant more of his weight onto her breasts. 'Please!' she sobbed, the cry torn from her throat, but the pressure grew, the pain more.

Leah tried to bear it, knowing her efforts would please him, perhaps even arouse him. She clung to the tattered remnants of her pride as her breast was crushed beneath his heavy sole. 'Master!' she cried at last, surrendering with a sob of shame.

He withdrew his foot and knelt beside her, his movements liquid, almost unnoticed. He reached for her, for the chain between the clamps biting into her nipples. He hooked a finger idly beneath it and pulled upward, stretching her nipples and causing pain to flare. His other hand lowered the zipper of his trousers and momentarily slipped inside, emerging with his manhood. It was flaccid but still large, and as she watched he began to harden.

He pulled on the chain again, tugging her numbed nipples, then gave a sudden tug and Leah cried out. His cock lengthened, and then he tugged again on the chain and she screamed. He was pulling her torso up by her nipples, pulling her face closer to his erection. The pain made her writhe and arch desperately, trying to ease the pressure until, as she realized his intent, she could slip her lips around the swollen glans of his erection, which sank into her mouth as she frantically licked and sucked.

His eyes caught hers and a wave of primitive hunger washed over her, and she shuddered as she strained her head up and took his cock deeper. He was using her, and no matter what shame she felt she would grovel to feel that terrible, wonderful sexual rush through her veins. It was worse than any narcotic, the pleasure more fantastic, more intoxicating, and more addictive than anything mere mortals could conceive of. But then he was no mere mortal. He was no mortal at all.

163

His fingers were long and slender, strong enough to crush metal. They slid through her tangled hair and pulled gently. His cock thrust down into her throat, and Leah gurgled in dazed and overwhelming passion. Her face was pressed against his groin, her lips tight around the base of his cock, her nose pressed into his nest of black pubic hair.

His grip loosened, then tightened, loosened, then tightened, guiding her face up and down on his cock. His hips began to move, thrusting against her using athletically economical movements, his cold dark eyes holding hers. Being used so indifferently made her begin to tremble violently, sexual hunger consuming her, tensing her muscles, her traitorous sex yearning to be penetrated.

His hips continued to work rhythmically, his cock sliding easily up and down as he fucked her flushed, perspiration beaded face. Then he pulled back, slowly withdrawing his long thick cock until the bulbous head lodged between her stretched lips, and then with no indication of emotion he came and hot, viscous liquid filled her mouth. It burned her tongue and her palette, and set her throat on fire as she desperately swallowed the copious ejaculation.

Convulsions wracked her tortured frame and she shook more and more violently as he permitted her to orgasm too. But she knew it was only the prelude to the ecstasy he would give her – if he chose to.

His hands moved over her, but she hardly noticed them until suddenly the clamps were gone from her nipples, the chain unattached from her clitoral ring, her stiff legs straightening a little as the chain binding her ankles to her sex receded with a slight scraping sound on the attic floorboards.

Agony seized her nipples as the circulation returned, and tears filled her eyes and spilled down her cheeks as she held her position, her body trembling, her lips still tight around the head of his placid cock as she adored it greedily, desperate for every drop of his essence.

But then he drew back. 'Have you had enough of me?' he asked, his question caressing her weary body like soothing velvet. He was taunting her and she knew it, ashamed she could not resist him, could not control herself in his presence.

'Please,' she begged, abandoning all pretenses to pride and strength. 'Please use me as you will, master.' She licked his polished boots. Her wrists and ankles were still shackled, but she could move to some degree now and did so, her tongue lapping desperately at his boots, kissing the pristine leather in adoration. Shame and self-retribution filled her, but the despair she would feel if he turned away was too great a threat to contemplate.

'Then assume the position,' he said.

Shocked with an intoxicating blend of excitement and trepidation, Leah twisted and awkwardly pulled her aching body onto her knees. She took her weight on her forearms and raised her bottom for him, spreading her knees as wide as she could with her ankles still shackled together. Her hairless sex strained for him from between her toned thighs, her labia swollen with hunger, her clitoris glistening, her juices coating her sex and the insides of her thighs as she trembled and waited anxiously, terrified he would abandon her. Nothing else mattered. She was consumed with her desire for him.

And then she heard him move and felt him against her, felt the spongy head of his revitalized penis pressing against her exposed entrance. He was too large, he always was. He hurt her as he thrust and penetrated her, but then he always did.

It was ecstasy as he filled her, the moist, velvet sheath

of her sex stretching to accommodate him. And then he began to move. Every deep, savage stroke sent a wave of pleasure flooding through her core. Her eyes widened in wonderment and her lips parted in a soundless, breathless scream of fulfillment, the pleasure so intense she felt humbled.

He fucked her dispassionately, his groin slapping against her upraised buttocks, his fingers digging into her flanks with bruising force, his cock pumping cruelly into her cunt as she quivered beneath him. Naked and chained, sweat coating her rocking body, she had been reduced to a mindless creature of carnal hunger. Her ass thrust back eagerly, her insides spasming around the rigid cock pounding back and forth within her. Passionate groans spilled from her lips as her storm of pleasure rose to a crescendo, and she screamed, exhausted and breathless, her cries of unrelieved passion filling the attic space.

'What are you?' The question emerged as a fatigued croak as Leah knelt before him.

He shrugged. 'Any answer I give you will sound clichéd or too incredible for you to absorb.' She continued to stare inquisitively at him, and he smiled faintly. 'Very well,' he conceded, 'I am a vampire.'

Leah felt ice chill her spine at the confirmation. 'But that's impossible,' she whispered, her voice unsteady.

'Of course it is.'

'If there are vampires,' she went on, unconvinced by her own denial that such things existed, 'why isn't it more commonly known?'

'Because,' he said as if speaking to a child, 'anyone who reported one would be instantly ridiculed and probably deemed insane.'

'But surely the authorities…'

'Go and tell a doctor or a police officer that a vampire has bitten you. See how far you get.'

Leah stared at him helplessly.

'There are always logical answers to whatever puzzles my people leave lying around, including someone deliberately trying to fool the authorities with macabre damages to bodies. Besides, it's not that difficult to make humans forget, to fog their memories, or simply to implant a suggestion that will cause them to ignore certain things. In the event someone did actually suspect something was amiss he or she would very quickly forget his concerns after a brief conversation with me or someone like me.'

She looked at him for a long moment, knowing he was right. 'How long, I mean, how many...?'

'We have always been few,' he told her, knowing her question before she'd completed it. 'There are perhaps ten vampires of power in the US, and four or five times that many younger ones of less influence and power.'

He reached for her and gripped her hair lightly but insistently, pulling her up to her feet and forward until she straddled him. Incredibly he was already erect again, and he maneuvered her over his erection and then down, and Leah could not suppress a grateful sigh as he forged up inside her.

Despite clearly being aroused again he apparently felt no real urgency, for he held her still on his lap, gently kissing her breasts and nipples, his hands moving up and down her back as she sat motionless, impaled upon his sturdy column of flesh.

'W-why aren't there bodies of your victims everywhere?' she gasped, unable to leave the conversation alone despite the pleasure trying its best to distract her.

He shook his head and stroked her fringe off her brow with what felt like real affection. 'We don't need to kill,

167

my dear. That's a myth created by ignorant writers. Do you think I could drink all the blood in a human body at one sitting? Please. A pint or so does me nicely for a day or two, and it's not at all difficult to obtain.'

He curled his little fingers through her nipple rings and tugged repeatedly so that her nipples hurt again, but she cared not. It was hard to keep concentrating with the longing rousing within her once more, with the hunger beginning to grow again. Yet she'd been aroused to one degree or another for so long now that she'd learned to function after a fashion, and she was desperate to find out what was happening to her.

'Those vampires at the nightclub…' she pressed, 'did they…?'

'I expect so,' he answered, again showing an aptitude for understanding a question even though it remained incomplete. 'You spoke of how weak you felt, so I presume they fed.'

Leah shuddered with dread.

'It did you no harm,' he went on, with a frightening casualness. 'And it wasn't as if they could ask you, now was it?' He looked amused by his own rhetorical question.

'Why the… the rings?' she whispered, the fingers at her nipples and the erection buried deep within her making it difficult to concentrate her thinking.

He smiled. 'We like to mark our favorites,' he explained. 'The rings possess power. We can speak to your body as well as your mind. It helps to ease the pain of our feeding. And there are spells which will aid in healing and changing the body.'

'Spells?' she gasped. 'You mean, like magic?'

'You may call it that,' he said, his hands gently caressing her back as he bent to nip lightly at her breasts. 'There are a variety of powers at play in this world, and some of us are able to manipulate them in ways we find helpful.'

He smiled. 'Sexual heat and need, physical and sexual pleasure, are the opium in which we deal. It seduces our prey and makes them feel unconcerned with what we do. The more sexually responsive a person is the easier they are to sexually please, and thus to control.'

'But I... I don't want anyone controlling me,' she protested.

'Of course you don't,' he said placidly, his fingers kneading her bottom.

'So why me?' she gasped.

'Why you?' He stroked his chin thoughtfully. 'Chance, luck, beauty, strength of will and character. Do you think all blood tastes alike and has the same qualities? I assure you that it does not. People are like wine, and each is slightly different. Male and female blood tastes different, as does young and old. And your blood is a particularly fine vintage.'

His fingers squeezed beneath her buttocks and lifted her as though she were weightless, then dropped her down. Leah cried out, her thoughts abandoned as his stiff cock filled her again, shuddering weakly as she tried to hold on to her sanity. She realized he was right. When she was feeling this much sexual need it was virtually impossible to care about anything else.

His hands lifted her again and her head rolled from side to side, her back arching as his rigid shaft rasped across her swollen clit. There were so many questions she wanted to ask, so many things she wanted to say, and yet... none of them mattered at all.

She sank back down with a cry of delight and the muscles in her thighs began to tense, trying to push herself back up once more, but he chuckled and held her in place to taunt her, biting lightly her breasts and nipples as she squirmed and moaned.

Then he lifted her up and down in rapid motions, bouncing her on his lap several times, then held her still again as she swayed, close to fainting. 'P-please…' she gasped.

He chuckled, and then pushed her back so that her torso was parallel to the floor and her hair swept it, one hand moving casually across her taut front, over her full breasts and stiff nipples, then across her hollowed belly and between her legs, where his fingers massaged her clitoris. With her hands still shackled behind her there was little Leah could do as he played her body like a classical pianist, creating music within her soul.

He lifted her back upright and she swayed dazedly. His hands again squeezed beneath her bottom, lifting her until with a sigh of disappointment she felt his erection slip out of her tightly clutching sex. He turned her over his lap, running his hands over her bottom then between her thighs, gently stroking her sopping sex.

'There are so many more interesting things you can do with your limited life than hunt after criminals,' he said, his fingers kneading her buttocks. 'You were made for feeling so much more pleasure than you have ever yet experienced.'

She felt a finger circle the wrinkled bud of her anal opening, then draw back, and a moment later his hand cracked down across her bottom, making her jerk on his lap.

'As one cannot truly accept the wonder of summer without winter, so one cannot revel in pleasure without knowing pain.'

He spanked her again, and then again, sharply slapping her upturned bottom, pain flaring through her pelvis, her clitoris gleefully absorbing it. Then a moment later two slender fingers drove deep into her sex and she stiffened, crying out in bliss.

She heard him chuckle, and then felt another sharp slap across her bottom, then another, and another. 'P-please,' she sobbed, her head flung back as three fingers thrust sharply into her sex, pumped swiftly in and out, then withdrew. Another crack of pain burned through her, and another as he resumed the spanking.

'Heat,' he said. 'The heat of pleasure, the heat of pain.' He caressed her bottom, skimming lightly over the blotchy red marks, then lifted his hand and spanked her again. Then Leah felt a finger touch her anus again, this time pushing insistently, twisting from side to side as the pressure forced the tight opening to yield and the straightened digit sank within.

'It's a matter of training the body as well as the mind,' he said, his free hand still spanking her, alternating from one buttock to the other, around the stationary hand the stiffened finger of which penetrated her rectum.

He moved that stiffened finger slightly, and Leah felt the pressure grow against her anal passage as a second finger squirmed in to join the first, both pumping slowly in and out of her rectum as she groaned and squirmed in helpless need.

He shifted her body back off his thighs so that she knelt on the floor beside him, stretching his arm to keep his fingers inside her ass, her breasts squeezed against his thigh, and with her face over his groin he fed her his erection. She swallowed it hungrily, her lips smoothing up and down before descending fully, engulfing the entire column, gurgling weakly as it penetrated her throat.

He ran his fingers through her hair as her lips remained pressed around its base, then tugged, lifting her face insistently. And then his hand closed around her neck and he forced her back down all the way, pressing her face into his groin and holding her there. Leah heard him whispering something, almost chanting in a language she had never heard before and certainly did not understand.

She almost choked and tried to lift her head, but he held her easily in place as his erection pulsed in her mouth and throat. He gripped her hair, pulling her head up then thrusting it down again. He began to grind his hips and maneuver her mouth to please himself and Leah gurgled helplessly, the fingers still impaling her rear as he fucked her throat, tipping her over into another blissful orgasm.

Chapter Thirteen

'Are you going to keep me like this?' Leah asked, but he merely looked down at her and smiled. 'Why are my wrists shackled?' she asked plaintively. 'Are you afraid of me?'

'Afraid of you?' He chuckled and shook his head. 'No, I just like the helplessness of bound women. But if it pleases you…' He waved a hand and the bands around her wrists felt suddenly cold and her arms dropped away from each other. She moved them round to her front and tried to rub some feeling back into her numb wrists.

'Isn't there something you would like me to wear?' she tried again.

'You're wearing all any woman needs to,' he said.

'I've been up all night,' she said wearily. 'I'm tired.'

'Of course you are, and there's a bed made up for you along the hall.'

'But it's almost dawn,' Leah pointed out unnecessarily. 'I have to be in work today.'

'You don't need to work anymore,' he said, looking amused.

'But I… I want to,' she said.

His eyes narrowed. 'And I can make you not want to very easily, young lady.'

'So do you want another mindless toy like them?' Leah challenged, nodding over her shoulder at one of the shaved girls kneeling by the door. 'I thought you wanted something more than that with me.'

His eyes grew cold for a moment, but then he smiled.

'Indeed I do,' he agreed, 'and I should not then complain that my little toy has a mind of its own. Very well, you may go out and play police officer.'

'I'm not playing,' she said indignantly, the rings in her nipples and clitoris instantly becoming hot and she gasped, clutching at them, wincing at the burning sensation against her sensitive flesh.

'Do not contradict me,' he calmly warned her. 'I will allow you a little impertinence from time to time, it amuses me, but I will not tolerate defiance.'

'I'm... I'm sorry,' Leah apologized, feeling like a naughty little girl again.

'You will learn your place,' he said, both with confidence and prophecy.

'What is my place?'

He smiled. 'You see my pets?' He gestured to the shaved girls kneeling nearby, and Leah swallowed, feeling a twisted rush of fear and excitement.

'Am I to be one of them?' she asked.

'No,' he said. 'One reason being because I like your lovely hair.'

'But what about their minds?'

'Would it make you feel any better if I told you they were each violent murderers?' he asked, shocking her.

Leah stared at the girls, then at him. 'Were they?'

He smiled. 'No. They were initiates in a convent, set to become nuns. Such a waste that would have been. So lovely, so responsive, and yet doomed to chastity forever. A priest tried to kill me and so after I killed him I took them as a, um, payment from his church.'

'W-what did you do to their minds?' Leah asked cautiously.

'Oh, nothing special,' he said airily. 'This was well over a hundred years ago, you know. They were ignorant

174

peasant girls in rural Poland. Easily influenced.'

'Over a hundred years ago?' Leah stared at the girls, none of whom looked out of her teens.

'What was done to them halted the aging process,' he answered her unspoken question.

'Like it did with you?' she probed.

'In a sense, yes. Their lives are bound to mine, of course. If I die, so do they.'

'And... and what about me?'

He smiled and fondled her breast, and Leah swooned with pleasure. 'You will feel more energy, more power, have more resilience. No doubt you have already noticed it, already noticed how much more soft is your skin and hair, how much more alert you are, how little sleep you require. Your bruises and other hurts will fade much faster, and no disease will overcome you.'

'And will I die if you do?'

'Some day – once you have passed your normal lifespan. If I were to die now? No. In twenty years? No, but you would age very rapidly, twenty years in a few moments. In a century? Yes.'

'Are you saying I'm to live forever?' She gaped at him.

He smiled and rolled her quivering nipple between thumb and forefinger. 'My dear, no one lives forever,' he said urbanely. 'But you might live a very long time by mortal measures.'

She turned and looked at the girls again. 'But not like that?'

'I have enough mindless, voiceless pets,' he said derisively. 'I require something more. More intelligence. Someone more... animated.'

'Someone to talk to.'

'Loneliness?' he asked with a wry smile. 'No, I am not lonely, but yes, I do want someone capable of talking to me, on occasion.' He smiled and thrust a finger into her sex and Leah cried out, arching her back. 'On occasion,' he said.

The worst part was that she loved him. She knew it was not real, but it was no less strong for having been forced upon her. And the sexual hunger was intense, whatever the cause, and would not be denied.

When she woke she found two thin chains attached to her nipple rings. Just as the rings had no apparent opening, neither did the chains. They led up to her collar, attached there with no means of removal she could detect. Their length was precise, just enough when she stood, to pull her nipples ever so slightly up, to provide a constant tug on them.

Of course, when she moved her breasts quivered slightly, and the pull of the chains on her nipples was a constant rhythmic reminder. It took very little walking before her nipples both ached and she found herself surreptitiously stroking her breasts as illicit pleasure flooded her body.

The ring through her clitoris held a small weighted ball not much larger than a marble, but it was a spiked ball, an irritant that rubbed against her exquisitely sensitive button with every movement.

Yet whenever Morales appeared she felt a wave of adoration and unendurable lust that had her on her knees crawling to him, shamed by her responses but desperate for his attention. And then the inevitable orgasms, when they came so predictably, were so shattering she was left breathless and dazed.

It could not be fought. She gave up trying. Trying to hate him was pointless. Trying to fight him painful and useless. Instead she tried to find some type of accommodation for herself as his sex toy. And to understand the creature who now had such control over her.

She was responsible for looking after the shaven girls he kept in his basement. They lived in cages, and lived only to serve and let their bodies be used. At first she tried talking to them, but that proved fruitless. They did not speak and ignored whatever she said unless it was an order to do something. They always smiled benignly, and seemed even hornier than she was.

It was almost as difficult to deal with them as it was with Morales, for while they did not affect her as he did they tried to get their hands and lips onto the more sensitive parts of her body, and that very quickly did the job of disabling whatever intelligence she had as her body turned to fire at their expert touch. Let one of those cunning tongues slide wetly across her skin too often and she would dissolve into a puddle of sexually desperate flesh. Let their tongues touch her between the legs and it was instant meltdown.

So she had to be very stern and careful around them, snapping at them, gesturing, slapping their bottoms whenever they tried to lick or grope her or were slow to obey. They were fed and watered as one would a dog, by placing bowls of food and water on the floor of their cage, or wherever they were at any given time. Sometimes they would eat in the kitchen.

Bathing them involved having them kneel on all fours and then washing them as quickly and chastely as possible before her own desires melted her determination and her fingers began to stroke too long over fragrant pussies or caress soft, soapy breasts.

Often as not she gave in when washing them and was soon writhing on the floor with one or more soapy girls sliding against her. During one such ablution session her heat was already up when Morales appeared, along with the usual wave of lust, awe and devotion. Perhaps because she was already trembling with lust she was partly shielded from the shock of his presence, at least enough to speak intelligently.

'I thought you wanted more than a mindless toy,' she said, gasping at the lust within her. He cocked his head to one side, smiling lightly. 'I can't resist whatever you're doing. You might as well shave my head and make me into a whining, simpering beast, because that's all I am around you anyway.'

She dropped to her knees and licked his shoe as if to demonstrate, yet there was real pleasure in it and she moaned, her hips rolling.

'Do you think I do something special for you, my sweet?' he asked in amusement, reaching down to grip her hair and pull her head up. 'This is what it feels like to be in my presence. You felt it your first night here. Of course, now your body is much more attuned to your sexuality, and your mind has lost much of its inhibitions. However, I will see if I can, as you say, tone it down a little around you.'

Almost immediately the sense of awe and attachment began to recede. The sexual need did not, however, and she screamed in pleasure as he thrust himself into her.

But afterwards it was much more easy to speak to him without falling apart. 'I really have to go back to work,' she said.

'You took a couple of days off, ill,' he pointed out to her.

'I know.' She had called in sick in his presence, almost trembling with the desire to do his bidding, to make him happy. 'But my boss will start making trouble for me if I don't go back.' Of course there was no chance of hiding her relationship with Mbweni, and it soon spilled out into the open as he smiled encouragement.

'How interesting,' he mused. 'Such a woman could be of interest to me.'

'I'm not sure how your powers would effect a lesbian.'

He chuckled. 'I don't envisage any difficulties, but I'm certain you and my other little pets will do well for me if needed. Invite her over. We shall give her to the dogs for a while and then speak with her.'

'She's very strong willed,' Leah told him.

But he merely shrugged dismissively and said, 'Humans are never very difficult to sway.'

Mbweni glowered at Leah from the porch, but the glower disappeared as she noted Leah's state of undress.

'You never cease to amaze me, MacInnes,' she said, and reached out to finger one of the taut chains attached to her nipples, tugging it lightly, then glanced down and smiled, fingering the little spiked ball that rested against her clitoris. 'And who have you been keeping house for, hmmm?'

'Come in and I'll show you,' Leah invited.

'Why haven't you been at work these last two days?' Mbweni demanded.

'Come in and I'll show you,' Leah repeated.

Mbweni looked around warily, and then cautiously accepted the invitation to enter the foreboding house. 'Very well,' she said curtly, 'show me whatever it is you seem so keen to show me.'

Leah closed the front door and led her boss down the stairs and along the narrow corridor to where the girls waited, and when Mbweni saw them Leah was gratified to see even this ice-maiden's eyes widen and her mouth open in amazement.

'My, my, my,' she said, her voice low, her demeanor pensive. 'What a pretty little litter of kittens.'

'Kittens with soft tongues,' Leah said.

Mbweni smirked. 'And I bet you've experienced them all.' One of the girls caught her hand and licked it before she could draw it back. Another did the same with her other hand, and Mbweni stared down at them, confused and bemused. 'Friendly little girls,' she said. 'They're very into their slavery, aren't they?'

'Oh, are they ever,' Leah confirmed.

The third girl was licking Mbweni's boot, gripping her ankle as her tongue slipped wetly across the black leather. She pulled herself up Mbweni's body, and the tall black woman glowered at her, though clearly intrigued. 'What kind of game are you all playing?' she asked, her voice a little husky.

The girl kissed her before Mbweni could draw back, grasping her shoulders as she wormed her tongue into Mbweni's mouth. Mbweni stiffened, and then pushed her back instinctively. But her eyes seemed to lose focus and she stared around her as if mystified, her breathing growing heavier as the girls closed in.

'W-wait,' she panted breathlessly. The girls were sliding their hands over her body, pulling at her clothes, undoing buttons as their lips moved against hers, and against her throat. Her blouse was pulled open, her bra deftly unclipped and eased aside, and Mbweni shuddered as one of the girl's pressed her lips around her nipple and began to suck. 'Oooh…' she gasped, her eyes narrowing dreamily as her legs trembled.

And then sinuous bodies swamped her, their hands removing clothes and underwear and their tongues and lips devouring exposed flesh. Her legs were spread wide

180

and one of the girl's attached her mouth to her sex, and Mbweni cried out as she came, her back arching violently, her head lolling to the side.

Leah backed away, aroused but fighting it, then turned and hurried from the room, gasping for breath as she felt the heat easing somewhat.

'Well?' Morales looked up indolently.

'Mbweni is with the girls,' she told him.

'I trust she's enjoying herself.' He smirked. 'We'll speak to her later, perhaps tomorrow.'

'Yes, master,' Leah said meekly.

'In the meantime, let's go for a walk.'

'I love the city at night,' Morales said, inhaling deeply.

'Full of freaks and weirdoes,' Leah grumbled with a frown, her eyes turning warily from side to side as she walked along next to him.

'Some of my most interesting acquaintances,' Morales said with a smile, and Leah pulled a face. 'Yes, well, a thousand years of experience with humans has produced a degree of cynicism, too.'

'Humans aren't all crazed beasts,' Leah argued.

'I said nothing of crazed,' he pointed out. 'Humans want your body, my dear. They want to touch it, and instinctively want to fuck you, with a cock or a dildo it doesn't much matter. And why not? It's something that gives them immense pleasure, and only that thin mask of civility holds them back. But make no mistake, my dear, what goes on behind their eyes when you pass before them is more than just an appreciation of your lovely wardrobe.'

'You chose this dress,' she said resentfully. It was a slinky spandex mini-dress, barely low enough to cover her bottom and with a deep, plunging neckline which exposed much of her breasts.

'Oh, and it's far more revealing than what you wear to nightclubs,' he said sarcastically.

Leah pouted. 'That's different,' she sulked.

He took her hand in his. 'Would you like some insight into your fellow man?' he asked in a slightly patronizing tone.

'What do you mean?' she asked warily.

'What goes on behind those eyes that watch you?'

They passed a group of young men, and Leah didn't have to look to know their eyes were upon her. 'I don't need to know,' she murmured.

'You think you already know.'

'As much as I need to.' She felt a tingling run up her arm, and lurched briefly to one side. 'What did you do?' she asked in alarm.

'Nothing harmful, nothing permanent,' he assured her. 'You will see through my eyes, sense what I sense.'

'But I…'

Morales turned to look at a man they approached. He was nondescript, perhaps thirty, wearing brown trousers and a blue jacket. He did not appear to be looking at them. Then in an instant she was inside the man's head, as if floating lightly at the surface of his mind. He was concentrating on the road, waiting for a silver sedan. Then his eyes caught sight of her. She felt his interest jump, felt his eyes focus, run up and down her body, feast on her cleavage, dance away, then flick back. There was an awareness of Morales, and a wariness of being caught staring at 'his' woman. The eyes flickered, flitted. 'What a rack,' the man thought. 'Fucking nice body.' Her breasts were unveiled. She was bent over naked.

They passed him and she felt his head turn, felt his eyes crawl over her hips, then onto her bottom and thighs.

Again she was bent over naked, his hands cupping her breasts. Then the vision faded and he looked up the street again, waiting for the sedan.

'I don't...' Leah started, but faltered.

They passed another man, and another, and another. None appeared to take much notice of her on the outside. Yet behind their eyes she felt the bolt of lust within them each time they saw her, felt their eyes moving over her body, heard their appreciative thoughts on her hair, her face, her breasts, her ass, her legs.

I'd like to get my hands on those.

Man, what a piece of ass.

Nice lookin' bit of cunt.

There's a bitch needs fuckin'.

Woah! What a cutey!

I wish Stephanie would wear something like that.

Jesus, what a slut!

Niiiiice.

Bits and flashes of fantasies blossomed and faded like soap bubbles in the men they passed. Most of them were obscene and graphic. She saw images of herself on her knees fellating men, on her back with her legs spread, or on all fours being fucked from behind.

'S-stop this,' she gasped.

The images swarmed around her as they passed more men. Morales was sifting the surface thoughts of them all, and she was growing dizzy with their explicit words and graphic images.

It didn't matter who they passed, their age or station. Dignified men in suits, deliverymen in coveralls, lounging teenagers barely into adolescence, strung out heroin addicts, shop assistants, fathers with their families. It didn't matter. The worst was a group of young busboys lounging for a smoke outside a hotel. Their minds and eyes and

183

thoughts rolled over her, graphic and raw and hungry. It felt as if their minds were hands, clawing at her body and groping her everywhere.

Then it all faded into babble, and disappeared. She slumped weakly against him, shaken.

'Your fellow man appreciates your beauty,' he said with a smirk.

'Bastard,' she whispered, and jerked her hand away from him. 'You dressed me like this!'

'It would make very little difference if you were dressed in jeans and a T-shirt,' he said. 'They want you. It's both instinctive and cultural.'

'So men are all raving horny bastards.'

'Hardly raving, but yes to the rest.'

'But not you, of course,' she said sarcastically.

'I am somewhat more in control of myself. One cannot control the emotions of others unless one knows oneself.'

'You sound like a Chinese fortune cookie.'

'There is much wisdom in the Orientals.'

'Anyway, it's not right to – to control others' emotions, to play with them.'

'I decide what's right or wrong.'

'You are so arrogant. What gives you the right?'

'I have cause to be arrogant. And power gives me the right. It places me above mere mortals.'

'Mere mortals? Listen to yourself. Do you think you're God?'

He stopped walking suddenly at a bus stop. There were two young women there, and Leah watched as he spoke to one, then the other. Leah could see the girls swaying slightly, could remember the strange sense of falling, of melting as her eyes met his. She couldn't hear him, but could hear the smooth murmur of his silky voice.

He walked back to her and she saw the two young

women staring after him.

'What was that?' she asked.

He smiled mysteriously and led her along the street a little way, then stopped and turned and looked back. 'Samantha,' he said softly, 'and Christine. Samantha is the blonde.'

'What did you do to them?' she asked warily.

'They go to Cal Tech,' he said in an almost dreamy voice. 'They're so very young and earnest. And yet within them is desire, desire they are repressing for fear of how others may see them, fear of how each sees the other.'

The two girls looked to be no more than eighteen or nineteen. One had shoulder length blonde hair and rimless glasses, and wore a short blue dress beneath a long white sweater. The brunette's hair was in a ponytail. She wore white drawstring trousers and a multicolored T-shirt beneath a jean jacket.

The two began to whisper as they watched, then the brunette pushed the blonde back against the telephone pole bearing the bus stop sign and kissed her slowly and languorously. The blonde wrapped her arms around her friend and began to run her hands up and down her back. Their kiss became more passionate and the blonde's hands slid down onto the other girl's bottom, squeezing and kneading her buttocks through her trousers.

'I don't understand,' Leah said anxiously.

She watched the brunette, Christine, begin to fondle her friend's breasts through her sweater. The blonde, Samantha, pushed the jacket back over the brunette's shoulders, then peeled her T-shirt up and off.

'You're doing this!' Leah exclaimed.

'Not precisely, no,' he said in a soft voice filled with concentration.

'Stop it!'

185

'I'm not forcing them to do it. I'm merely raising the heat in their loins, in their bodies, in their minds. They want to do this. Each has had fantasies about the other but feared rejection. They simply don't care at this point who is watching or what happens. Their ardor is too intense for anything else to matter.'

There were several others at the stop, but they were paying no attention at all to the two, and Leah bit her lip as the brunette almost frantically tugged up the other girl's sweater and dropped it to the ground, then tore at her dress.

'They'll be arrested if someone notices,' Leah protested. She could hear their groans and gasps of pleasure now, and traffic was slowing to a crawl in front of them. Samantha's hand was down inside Christine's drawstring trousers, moving animatedly, and Christine was moaning and swaying and rolling her head from side to side. Suddenly the blonde tugged the trousers down completely. The brunette stumbled forward against her, pushing her back across a newspaper-vending box. She tore her dress down and off, then ripped her panties away and flung herself on top of her.

'Stop it,' Leah whispered, 'please!'

'I'm not a god,' he said with a smug smile.

'Doing this doesn't make you a god,' she said between clenched teeth.

Both girls were now entirely nude, their hands moving feverishly over each other's bodies, their lips crushed together as they writhed against the box. Then they slumped and sprawled across the sidewalk.

'What do you think it makes me?' he asked incuriously.

The blonde spread her legs and the two ground their bodies together, kissing and licking at each other's mouths. Samantha twisted her lower body as Christine pushed

186

herself back. Their legs scissored together as Christine leaned forward. Their hands joined and they began to grind their pussies together directly. Their cries of pleasure rose and passion and heat filled their faces.

'Why can no one see?'

'They can. They simply do not notice.'

'How?'

'A simple talent. I place a dull image in that place, an echo, a scent, a vision, and imbue it with power. Mortal eyes that look upon it see what I have placed there and nothing more.'

'Like me in the nightclub?'

'Yes.'

'Do all vampires do this when they're bored or playful?'

'It depends on how bored,' he said, turning dark eyes upon her, 'and how playful.'

'They said… one of them said I was marked. Was that why they chose me?'

He hesitated, and Christine cried out in her orgasm.

'Not all of us have the same strength, of course, and younger vampires have the least,' he explained. 'The mind of a human is putty in the hands of one of my age and power, but to the newly risen, well, it can be quite a challenge.'

'That doesn't answer my question,' Leah pressed.

The two girls rolled on the sidewalk, still kissing, still madly fondling and caressing each other. They twisted about so that their heads were between each other's legs and began to lick and tongue each other's pussies.

'Those who have been touched by one such as I have a… a glow about them which lasts for quite some time. They possess a heightened sexuality, as you are aware, and their minds are much more vulnerable, more open to further enhancement.'

'You mean they're much easier for others of your kind to take over,' she said bitterly.

'Crudely put.'

Both girls began to cry out in orgasm, their bodies twisting and bucking and grinding.

'So what you just did to those two will leave them vulnerable to any other vampires who come upon them, allowing them to be used as I was in the nightclub.'

He turned his dark eyes on her and smiled. 'And was it such a terrible experience?'

She glared at him. It had been a shocking, stunning, thrilling experience, one of the most fantastic of her life. 'But it's not up to you to do that without even asking!' she insisted vehemently.

'Very well.' He raised a hand and seemed to clutch at something, and almost immediately the two girls rolled apart. They cried out in shock, springing away from each other and staring around them, their eyes wide. Then they began to frantically scramble after their clothes, tugging them on as quickly as they could.

'Now instead of the joy and wonder they could have felt they will be left feeling shame and guilt,' he said. 'Are you content with that?'

Leah shook her head and he shrugged helplessly.

'You're an arrogant asshole!' she spat.

He frowned at her and his eyes narrowed. 'Beware of angering me, my sweet.'

Leah felt a sudden swelling heat within her body and tried to swallow her anger. 'You have no right to… to a-abuse… you s-stop this!' she gasped. The heat rose around her like a curtain, a sweltering heat that had her body trembling with need. 'B-bastard,' she panted, trying to keep her trembling hands away from her body – and his.

He smiled condescendingly. 'You may apologize at any

time.'

'F-fu-fuc… oh!' Her hands slid under the short hem of her dress and she arched her back as she felt her bare sex against her fingers. She stumbled back against the wall behind her, rubbing frantically at herself with one hand as she squeezed the other down the front of her dress to fondle and knead her breasts. She tore the top of the dress down, her breasts spilling free, and groaned as she sank to her knees on the sidewalk, squeezing and mauling herself. She bent forward, gasping, thrusting one, two, then three fingers into her pussy, pumping desperately as her climax neared.

Yet it hovered on the edge, a sliver away, and despite the terrible heat and need driving her she could not push herself across. Gasping, moaning, she pulled her head up and back and stared at him, understanding somehow that he was preventing her from climaxing. 'P-please!' she begged.

'Remove your dress,' he said calmly, and her hands tore at it, ripping it up and off. It brushed against the ankles of an old lady tottering by.

'Your climax is denied you,' he told her coldly.

'Please,' she whimpered, pumping furiously, four fingers inside her now.

'Do you acknowledge my power?'

'Yes!' she cried.

'My supremacy?'

'Yes,' she sobbed. 'Anything!'

'And you do apologize for your rudeness, of course.'

'Yes!'

'And will accept my punishment?'

'Yes! Please, please, master!' She had never felt a need so intense, so all consuming. She was feverish with the sexual pressure tearing through her body and mind. A group of young men walked by, talking about a football game. One detoured to her left, another to her right. None looked down at her in passing.

The orgasm burst within her. She screamed, thrown over onto her back. Her legs flopped aside as her body began to buck and heave, her back arching, her head rolling from side to side. Her fingers drove desperately into her pussy again and again as the power of her release set her nerve-endings spitting like live electrical wires and forced her muscles to spasm violently again and again.

A deliveryman stepped across her going one way, and a middle-aged couple skirted her flailing feet going the other. The final explosive surge of ecstasy tore her hands from her body and flung them up and back behind her so hard her knuckles cracked against the sidewalk. Her back arched so sharply her spine creaked, and then she went limp, drained, her breasts heaving.

A mother holding her child's hand strolled past her, the small girl skipping across Leah's outspread legs, singing softly to herself.

Leah felt a sudden flush hit her body, a shimmer of cold passing across the surface of her skin. She felt the breeze across her flesh, felt the small pebbles and bits of grit beneath her buttocks and back. She shuddered and moaned, gulping in air as she stared up into the night sky.

'Do not mistake my tolerance for weakness, child,' he said, standing over her. 'If I am angered you will come to regret it. Passion is not the only emotion I can raise in you. Now put on your dress.' He kicked the discarded dress against her body and her eyes opened slowly, then closed again. 'In one minute I will release the vision set on your body and those around you will see you as you are.'

Panic hit her but for long seconds her body failed to

react. Then she twisted over on her side. She gulped in air and put her hands flat against the sidewalk, pushing repeatedly until she was able to sit up, then lifting herself to her knees. She stared around, then clawed at her dress and pulled it against her.

'Thirty seconds.'

She tried to tug the dress over her head, but discovered she had it upside-down. She stumbled to her feet and turned it around, then tugged it over her head and shoulders and down around her waist. She folded the top back up, smoothing it over her breasts as he raised a hand and gestured.

'Just in time,' he said with a wry smile. He reached for her and she took his hand, trembling. He started walking along the sidewalk again, holding her arm in his, and Leah followed on shaky legs.

'Ah, my kind of store,' he said, and she looked up wearily and saw the glaring neon sign of a sex shop. 'Shall we go inside and see what perversions mere humans can invent?'

He did not wait for an answer, but led her inside.

Chapter Fourteen

She followed him inside, gaining more control over herself now as she recovered from the exertion of her lust.

The shop was busy, with more than six or so men prowling its cluttered aisles. Leah dropped her eyes, blushing, as they all looked at her.

'They think you're a slut,' Morales said indifferently, leading her further inside. And perhaps she was, which was the worst part. Knowing what was behind their eyes, the lurid thoughts they would be having, she squirmed and tried to keep Morales between she and them.

'Hmm, here's one almost as large as me,' he said smugly, picking up an enormous dildo. He held it out to her. 'Care to try it out?'

'No,' she hissed, flushing as other men nearby stared at them, but she felt the rings begin to burn and gasped. 'Master,' he said quietly. '*Master*,' she repeated more desperately.

'Louder,' he quietly urged, his attention on another large dildo which he turned this way and that in his manicured fingers, examining it as though it were a piece of antique porcelain.

'Master!' she pleaded, loud enough for the two nearest men to hear her. Thankfully the rings stopped burning, but her face grew hotter with humiliation instead.

He picked up a vibrator and played with it, smiling at her, then activated it and pressed it against a nipple through her dress.

Leah gasped and jerked back, but he held her arm and rolled the buzzing toy in place, rubbing it back and forth across her nipple until she moaned softly, her body trembling. He chuckled, then slid it downwards, still holding her arm to keep her from backing away, sliding the shiny metal tube up beneath the short hem of her dress and pressing it against the little ball dangling from her clitoris.

'Oh!' she gasped, jerking and trembling. 'Please!'

More men were drifting closer, attracted by her and what Morales was doing, and she cringed with mortification. 'Please, master!'

'You have too much pride,' he calmly decreed. 'You need to lose some of it.'

Sex heat flared through her groin and up through her belly and chest. She moaned and twisted from side to side, gasping and biting her lip to keep from crying out.

'Take your dress off,' he ordered.

'Please,' she gasped. 'Please, no.'

'You forgot to call me *master* again,' he admonished impatiently. 'Your pride keeps getting in your way. Remove the dress.'

Shame was beaten down by the terrible sexual hunger gripping her body, and her hands shook as she reached for the hem of the dress and tugged it up, baring her naked sex and bottom, then her flat tummy, then her ringed nipples. With her face blazing she peeled it over her head and off, dropping it behind her.

Her rubbery legs stumbled and she fell back against a counter, her hands reaching for his as he rubbed the vibrator back and forth across her swollen sex. All the men in the store, including the proprietor, were watching with amusement and hunger.

But Morales would not let her orgasm, and so she could only tremble and writhe and moan and yearn. 'Please…'

she panted. 'Please, master…'

'Still too much pride.' He withdrew the vibrator and picked up the really large dildo, then pressed it against her sex, forcing it slowly up through the taut lips and into the moist channel of her belly. She groaned and shuddered, mortified that so many strange eyes were watching, yet unable to stop him, shaking with lust so badly her fingers were digging into the counter on either side to keep herself from masturbating right then and there.

The dildo slid deeper, achingly deep, painfully deep, and she could only groan and let her head fall back, staring at the ceiling as sweat beaded on her forehead.

Morales forced the dildo deep and left it in place, the last inch or so protruding from between her slick lips.

'Hands and knees,' he ordered abruptly, and whimpering she obeyed, dropping her eyes to the floor as all the men stared, sensing the murmur of hunger within them.

'Let us see what else we can find in this establishment,' he said, placing the vibrator aside with disinterest and proceeding further along the aisle, Leah obediently crawling beside him, the shame and humiliation burning her face even as the hunger made her body tremble with need.

'Ah,' he said, clearly pleased. 'We did speak about your punishment for impertinence, did we not?' He picked up a smooth flat strap, perhaps eighteen inches in length, rounded at the tip.

'Bend yourself across this counter,' he ordered, pulling her up by the hair until the pain forced her to her feet.

'Please,' she whispered, 'not hear. Please, I beg you, master.'

'Bend over the counter,' he sternly insisted, and disgraced she meekly obeyed, exposing her trembling lower body for them all, the dildo still protruding, the tight grip of her sex lips readily apparent to anyone watching.

He drew his arm back and the strap struck her bottom with a loud crack of noise and a sudden crack of pain. Leah gasped and rocked forward a little.

'Were you a bad girl?' he asked.

The strap again cracked across her bottom with stinging force.

'Yes, master!' she cried.

Again the strap cut across her buttocks, and again. The pain was intense and her bottom was quickly flaring and throbbing with heat.

The men gathered around, the evidence of their hardening cocks distending their trousers, staring rapturously at the lewdly displayed beauty as her bottom glowed red and the strap splatted across it repeatedly, a couple hungrily licking their lips, several openly rubbing their groins. They were ratty looking men in grubby clothes, none normally with a chance at a girl like her, men who were used to only watching them saunter past, fantasizing about what they would do to such a gorgeous female given half the chance.

'Are you sorry for being a naughty girl?' Morales asked mildly.

'Y-yes!' she squealed, but the strap bit loudly across her blotchy ass and she cried out again.

'Master,' he reminded her.

'I'm sorry, master,' Leah gasped, moaning as the strap bit into her aching bottom yet again.

'Are you a naughty girl?'

'Yes, master,' she conceded, knowing it was the correct response.

'Say it.'

She felt tears fill her eyes, partly from shame, partly from pain. 'I'm a naughty girl, master,' she said, her voice breaking, feeling his hand at her sex, gripping the dildo and forcing it even deeper, her fingers clutching the opposite edge of the counter as she held her breath.

'This,' he said, tapping the base of the dildo, 'belongs to me. But if anyone wants this,' he pressed his finger against her tight anus, 'it will cost him a dollar.'

She did not at first understand, and then she did and her face paled with shock as she heard and sensed the men crowd around her.

'Here's your dollar!'

'No, me!'

'Me first!'

'It's my shop. I get first go!'

Leah could not force herself to look around, but focused on one wall, trembling then gasping as the first of them moved behind her and began to grope her bottom. She felt his cock against her anus and closed her eyes, biting her lip as she felt the pressure increase. But her secret yearning was intense, and despite her shame she could not bring herself to resist, could not bring herself to tear herself away, to deny these animals what they craved, to say no and leave the seedy shop. It was not his mind controlling her, but her own body's hunger, and it craved the ugly sex she was about to be subjected to.

Leah stiffened as she felt the man's rigid cock penetrating her, sinking into her rectum. She was tight, but he penetrated her with a few determined grunts and shoves, and began fucking her ass with zero regard for her, as though she was no more than one of the dolls he sold to some of his more desperate customers. She smelt beer on his breath as he panted heavily over her shoulder and squeezed his grimy hands beneath her to maul her breasts, squeezing roughly.

'What about her mouth?' she heard one of them demand.

'I'll give you a dollar for that, too.'

'Oh, her mouth is worth far more than one dollar,' Morales said, 'because she has long mastered the art of taking a man into her throat. An extra ten cents, at least.'

A movement behind her, rough hands on her body, in her hair, and she twisted sideways, still leaning over the counter at an angle, but her head was turned around. She saw the man's cock protruding from the fly of his jeans, and then the head was rubbing against her lips as his fingers gripped her hair and forced her face closer still.

His cock slid into her mouth and she sucked hungrily, ashamed but wildly aroused as it forged across her tongue and stretched her lips wide. She moaned around it as he pumped in and out, and then braced herself as he pushed it deep and the head slipped down her throat.

Their hands roamed hungrily over her body, groping and squeezing as they cursed softly and used her. When the man behind her emptied his spunk into her ass another hurriedly took his place, and as he rutted into her she felt her hunger explode. She screamed silently, her body writhing and bucking as the orgasm flooded her.

She was left dazed, hardly aware of her surroundings for a brief period, and she didn't know how she came to be on the floor on all fours, nor cared as two men fucked her mouth and her ass. She felt drained of all energy, staring dully at the man's groin as he thrust inside her throat again and again.

Men who'd taken their turn with her weary body slouched around recovering, and others entered the shop, swelling their numbers, the little bell clanging dully each time the door opened and closed. And each newcomer, seeing the raunchy sight, maneuvered for their go at the submissive beauty.

Leah did not see Morales anymore, did not feel him.

When the latest man to ejaculate in her mouth released her hair she turned her head, still rocking forward as the man fucking her ass continued to stab his groin against her beaten buttocks, and saw no sign of him, feeling a sudden stab of fear, of abandonment. Then another men crowded her vision and eagerly thrust his cock into her mouth, holding her hair for surety as she began to suck.

She was used again and again, her body twisted and positioned just as the rabble wanted her. The dildo was extracted and she cried out in disgraceful delight as someone thrust his cock into her cunt from behind, her anus left unattended for the moment.

Then she was on her back, legs spread, knees forced back against her breasts as a fat man rammed himself down into her pussy. Then she was bent over the counter, fucked by a tattooed man with long unkempt hair. Then she was sitting astride a man slouched in a low chair, another thrusting into her bottom, a third holding her hair and pumping his erection in and out of her mouth and throat.

Orgasm after orgasm lashed her body and soul until she was little more than a dazed wreck, crying out for the next cock. She knelt, someone kneeling behind her, thrusting again into her rectum and squeezing her breasts, biting at the nape of her neck. A man stood before her, pumping his cock savagely into her mouth, his fingers clamped tight in her hair. Both her hands were stretched out to either side, pumping up and down on slick male erections as sperm spilled out over her fingers. Semen sprayed her face and hair and her breasts until she lay exhausted, drained, covered in sweat and male juices and looking up at Morales.

'Time to go home, I think,' he said, lending her enough energy to rise on shaky legs, and then he led her out of the shop. She left her dress and her shoes behind, forced to pad naked alongside him on the cold concrete. It was late, although she had no idea how long she had been in the shop. All the others had closed and the streets were largely empty. Still she squirmed, her arms folded over her breasts as she passed occasional pedestrians, but they took no note of her and she knew Morales was withholding the sight of her from them. Her feet were cold on the sidewalk, but she did not complain as she walked a little behind her master.

'Now let's see how your boss has been doing while we were away,' he said as they at last reached his house.

Mbweni, it emerged, had been enjoying herself rather too much. Left to the mercy of the girls she was exhausted by her own orgasms, exhausted to the point of unconsciousness, her complexion pale, her features drawn.

The girls, however, were insatiable and continued to play with each other, sighing as they writhed together.

'Put my pets in their cages before they wear themselves out completely,' he said with a wry smile. 'I'll put Mbweni to bed and let her recover somewhat before we talk.'

Leah did as instructed, leading the girls to their cages by their collars, while Morales carried Mbweni away as if she were weightless, but soon returned.

'She and I will talk when she wakes,' he said. 'Now as to you, I did promise you a punishment for your poor behavior.'

'I... I thought I'd already been punished,' Leah protested nervously.

'By enjoying all that sex?' he mocked. 'Oh no, that was merely to soften up that starchy pride of yours a little. No, your punishment must be something a deal less pleasant for you. But I am not without mercy, so you will have pleasure even in your pain.'

A black hole abruptly appeared in the wall behind him and he gripped her firmly by the arm and hauled her past him into it.

For long moments she fell through blackness, with no sight, no smell and no sound but her own screams. And then, abruptly, she stopped. She did not hit bottom, she was not caught. She was simply in another place.

And it was cold.

It was dark but she could see, after a fashion. She was outside – somewhere. Cold gnawed at her flesh and bones as she lay on a sheet of ice. She pulled herself up with a cry of discomfort. Freezing wind swirled around her and she clutched her arms to her breasts, her teeth already chattering as she stared around her.

There was no sign of a door, no sign of a building, or even a tree where she could shelter. She was in the middle of an endless sea of ice, with nothing in sight as far as the eye could see. The only sound was the mournful howl of the wind as it whistled around her, and her body felt cut by it as she danced from foot to foot.

Snow began to fall, getting heavier by the second. The wind picked it up and flung it sideways, spattering her face and body. 'I'm sorry!' she screamed, her voice barely audible even to her over the howling wind. She had never felt so cold in her life, never imagined it was possible to feel so cold. She sank to her knees on the ice, shivering vigorously, holding herself desperately.

'I'm sorry!' she cried again. Her flesh was freezing, her hands and feet numb, her breasts aching from the cold. It seeped deeper into her body and she felt herself growing stiff, frozen in place, but she continued to endure the terrible cold even as her limbs froze and she became almost a living statue, kneeling on the chilling ice.

The cold flayed her with its terrible icy bite. She felt her bone and muscle and internal organs freezing solid as the wind screamed shrilly past her ears. Her skin was white with frost and snow, and a layer of ice began to build on top of it, virtually entombing her alive.

She felt something beneath her shift. She could not move her head without great effort, and not enough to see beneath her. But she felt something solid pressing upwards against her groin, against the frozen lips of her sex. New pain assailed her as it forced her frozen labia aside and slowly drove upwards into her belly. It was cold, gleaming ice, and she cursed him in her mind, nearly hysterical with the unendurable cold.

It rose deep within her core; remorseless in its smooth movement until she knelt impaled upon it, feeling it burning her insides, the pain of its icy touch clawing at her insides.

There came another harsh touch, and another stout ice cock slowly forced its way through the frozen rosebud of her anus. Somehow, despite how utterly cold she was, the ice was still colder, rising into her tight rear channel, bloating, aching, burning, freezing.

And still the wind howled, icy blasts buffeting her, and the icicles inside her began to move, to stroke up and down within her. And they were melting, slick, wet, the water trickling from her anus and sex as they pumped in and out. Yet they did not melt away, they grew no more slender, no shorter, no smaller.

The cold was beyond intense and yet, despite it, despite her fear, despite her pain, the sensation of movement began to arouse her, although it was a different arousal to anything she had ever experienced before.

And yet, it seemed, pleasure could be cold as well as

hot, and so her freezing, trembling body felt an icy wash of sensual excitement, lust and desire and need racing through her. Were she not frozen stiff she would have been riding up and down on the pumping ice cocks. Yet they made up for her own lack of movement, thrusting deep into her body with long, hard strokes.

Pleasure rose, frosty, clawing at her mind. The wind howled, buffeting her freezing body, sending new chills through her even as the coldest sexual pleasure she had ever felt rippled up through her belly. The orgasm was intense and like none that had gone before, shattering like ice crystals pounded on an anvil by a sledgehammer.

The wind grew even more intense. It was not possible to survive such cold, not for more than a few minutes, but somehow every minute was as if it were her first, and the depth of the cold never seemed to diminish.

Another orgasm washed over her, even more raw, more intense, more powerful, and she screamed soundlessly, her body stiffening still further, vibrating like a tuning fork. And then somehow she was released, released to fall onto her back on the slick ice, crying out, her voice free once more as she squirmed, rubbing her sex and arching her back.

She went limp, exhausted, yet the sexual desire did not fade, it merely dimmed. She rose to her knees, still cold to her bones, folding her arms across her breasts. Her body was no longer covered in ice, no longer frozen; her skin was soft and warm again, yet she was freezing in the icy blasts of wind.

She slowly battled her way across the ice, her head turning from side to side, searching desperately for something, anything that would shield her from the terrible elements. And there, she spotted something. She hurried over, bending against the howling wind and gasping each time her bare feet pressed down on the cold ice.

She halted before a large frozen block. It was not shapeless; it was a perfectly carved figure of a large man with a very large and erect cock. She hurried forward, crouching next to the ice figure, hoping it could shield her, at least a little, from the savage wind.

Leah screamed as fingers entwined in her hair and she was pulled up, and her mouth opened in a cry of disbelief as she saw the carved face smiling at her. She was pulled closer by the icy fingers and desperately grasped the wrist in a futile attempt to wrench herself free. She cried out again as another hand of ice clamped around her thigh, freezing her terribly. And then she was being pulled over the thing, straddling it, and she moaned in denial as her body was lowered onto its enormous icy prong.

Terrible icy cold filled her belly, and pleasure followed it.

This was a bad dream, she told herself, it had to be. She was probably in Morales' house and this was all playing out in her mind. But she was no warmer for the thought, nor could she fight off the terrible excitement that gripped her.

The iceman released her thighs, his freezing hands rising to cup and squeeze her breasts so that she cried out. She came with a shriek that rivaled the howling wind, riding the thing's ice cock as she hungrily forced her pussy up and down.

Hours passed and eventually she was exhausted, and could only tumble off, crawling weakly, then lying down upon the ice. She awoke in bed, curling up into a secure ball, the memories of the frozen wasteland still strong.

'Bastard,' she muttered through clenched teeth.

She felt him calling her, and though she scowled she rose from the bed, no longer particularly concerned about her nudity as she walked through the house to where she knew he was waiting.

And as she arrived she saw Mbweni waiting with him. That was not entirely unexpected, though she wondered just how long she had been in the ice wilderness to allow Mbweni to have seemingly completely recovered from her sexual exhaustion.

She felt wariness lurking as she entered the room, sensing their moods, noting the look of satisfaction on their faces and in their eyes as they watched her. She had thought Mbweni would be made simply another of his playthings, perhaps one whose influence Morales could use, but Mbweni was dressed again while she, of course, remained naked, as Morales preferred.

'Ah, my pretty girl,' he said. 'Your boss and I have been discussing you, and what services she can perform for me.'

'Some new ones for her, I bet,' Leah said cynically.

Mbweni's eyes narrowed, but the look of satisfaction on her face only seemed to deepen, which made Leah even more wary.

'No, I do not seek those particular services,' Morales said. 'I have you and my pets for that. What need have I for another?' He looked at Mbweni and his smile deepened. 'Though of course, if I require those services of her she will be happy to perform them.'

Mbweni nodded, but with little enthusiasm.

'You may test your new power,' Morales said to her, and Mbweni moved towards Leah, who took an uncertain step back. 'Stay where you are,' he admonished Leah. 'She will not hurt you.'

'Your master and I have come to an agreement,' Mbweni

said, her tone stern. 'I will be his eyes and ears in the police department.' She let a fingertip lightly brush back the blonde hair over Leah's brow. 'And in exchange he has made me a gift.'

She smiled mockingly, and then eased back a step, raising her hands to Leah's breasts. She pressed the pads of her thumbs and forefingers to either side of Leah's nipples and squeezed, rolling the pink buds between them. The effect was slow, but impossible to ignore. As the seconds ticked by Leah's nipples began to tingle and throb, and she felt a growing frustration, a need to have them suckled and licked and bitten. Her breasts rose and fell more quickly as her breathing became more ragged. She fought to ignore the attention, but the sensations grew deeper and more profound so that her legs trembled and she could not repress her gasps and shudders. She could barely stop her hands from seizing the woman's and squeezing them between her thighs against her wet sex.

'I have given her that which my little pets have,' Morales said, 'but without the affect on her own mind. And I have extended it to her fingers. It is not quite as powerful, nor quite as instantaneous, for that might draw too many questions.'

Mbweni let her fingers spread out and gently cup Leah's aching breasts, caressing, leaving trails of fire in their wake, and Leah gasped helplessly, her head lolling back as her shoulders relaxed.

'Just think of how much pleasure I can bring to so many lovely girls with this,' Mbweni said, smiling like a sly fox, and then she leaned close, her tongue wet and glistening as she ran it across Leah's lips. Leah felt a sexual charge flood her mind, and dreamily returned the kiss.

But Mbweni moved back all too soon. 'And I am to be permitted to punish you for your impertinences,' she said.

'When your master is not using you I may do with you as I choose.'

The bands around Leah's wrists abruptly jerked back and snapped her arms together behind her, and Morales tossed a leash to Mbweni, the woman's smile feral now as she snapped the end of the leash to the ring piercing Leah's clitoris. 'Come with me, little slave girl,' she whispered.

Leah could do nothing else, nor really did she want to. She gasped as the woman tugged on the leash connected to her clit, but sexual need swamped her and she followed anxiously, casting an anxious glance back at Morales.

Chapter Fifteen

'How can you work for him?' she gasped, as Mbweni raised her arms and fastened her wristbands to chains dangling from the heavy brass posts flanking her.

'Why should I not?' Mbweni mused. 'He is power incarnate. I can use that power.'

'You're betraying your office.'

Mbweni laughed softly, shaking her head. 'Are you really that naïve? Do you think men of power don't influence the police force in everything it does?'

'And what are you going to do,' she demanded, fighting to control her inexplicable arousal, 'find defenseless girls for him to abuse?'

'Oh, hardly that,' Mbweni scoffed, gripped Leah's chin and jerked her face up to meet her own. 'I'm going to find defenseless girls for *me* to abuse.' She laughed in delight at her own wit, then dropped to her knees, spreading Leah's feet and snapping chains to her ankle bands.

'Aside from that all I need do is report anything to him in certain areas of interest,' she went on, almost conversationally. 'He does not like to be caught by surprise, so if I run across a pretty young thing whose just right for him...' she straightened with a smile, 'as you are, then I shall direct her to him.'

She began to gently caress Leah's breasts again. 'Besides, you betrayed me, young lady, betrayed me to a man you thought would abuse me with his nasty cock. And I shall punish you for such disloyalty.'

She let her fingers stroke idly down the curves of Leah's taut body, then trace up and down against the surface of her sex lips. Leah shuddered and her hips rolled helplessly, but Mbweni drew her fingers back, maintaining a very light pressure. Her tongue slipped into Leah's mouth tantalizingly briefly, then her teeth caught her earlobe and she nibbled delicately. The hunger within Leah built rapidly, becoming a desperate longing, and she felt her mind drowning in sexual need. Yet Mbweni drew back again and again, clearly enjoying herself as the girl began to moan and writhe in her bonds. Beads of perspiration stood out on her forehead, and on her breasts and back as she grew overheated. The urge to beg fought with her obstinate pride, and as one of the woman's fingers slipped just within the lips of her sex and sawed ever so lightly up and down she cried out helplessly, thrusting her hips forward in desperate frustration. But Mbweni merely drew her finger back so that the contact remained light and taunting.

'*Please*…' Leah pleaded.

'Poor dear, is there something you need?' Mbweni goaded.

Leah's body was glistening, her hair hanging moist around her shoulders, and then Mbweni edged back, studying her. She moved to a nearby oak table and picked up a very thin, light switch, moved around behind the captive girl, and with a decisive swing she brought the switch cracking across her vulnerable bottom.

Leah cried out at the stinging pain, her hips jerking violently forward, her head twisting back and forth. Yet she could do nothing to avoid the next blow, and the next, and the next, as the crop snapped across her bottom with precision blows that bit into her soft bottom like wasp stings.

The cruel blows began to push aside the sexual heat

permeating her insides, but only partially. It seemed nothing could entirely subdue that terrible need within her, though her bottom was soon a furnace of pain.

Then Mbweni was on her knees, her hands on Leah's hips, her tongue tracing the horizontal red lines of hurt that marked her buttocks, easing the pain, artfully turning the sting to pleasure instead. Her tongue moved upward, gliding up Leah's spine as the bound girl groaned and arched her back. She licked up behind her ear, then down across her shoulder and up her arm. Her tongue traced the delicate line of Leah's jaw, then dipped down between her breasts, circling her belly button, then gliding across her abdomen, bypassing her throbbing sex, lapping at her inner thighs instead.

Leah was soon even more overpowered by the hunger within her, frantic with need, but Mbweni moved away again, once more to the table, returning with a riding crop. It was heavier than the switch, and at its tip was a tiny triangle of leather. She let the crop move across the bedraggled girl's breasts and down her front, smiled and drew back her hand, then using only that soft tip swatted it against one of Leah's erect nipples.

The sensation was extraordinary, a mix of delicious pleasure and stinging pain produced by the extreme sensitivity of her body.

Mbweni began to punish her nipple with the implement, bringing it down in a flurry of blows that had Leah gibbering and writhing under the shockwaves of overpowering sensations. Mbweni then turned to the other nipple, striking it rapidly with the leather loop as well.

And then the woman dropped to her knees again, let her fingers ease between the wet lips of Leah's sex and ease them gently apart. So shockingly aroused was the trussed girl that her juices began to trickle slowly down her thighs.

Mbweni let her tongue lap upward against a trembling leg, and then eased her face forward and played her tongue between Leah's sex lips and across her clitoris, and Leah's eyes widened with delight as a shattering orgasm collapsed upon her.

'Feeling better?' Scott asked, and Leah nodded without speaking as they got into the car. He looked at her doubtfully. 'You've got dark rings under your eyes.

'I was sick,' Leah said abruptly. 'Let's leave it at that.'

'Well, we've made some progress on those missing girls, at least.'

Leah nodded. Mbweni had briefed her. It seemed Morales wanted the girls found as well, though neither had told her why. Leah suspected an acquaintance of his; some other person with odd strengths and powers was being too noisy, perhaps threatening to expose these people and their unnatural abilities. A younger, more careless vampire, perhaps?

But she found it difficult to really care. She was, to put it mildly, distracted. Now, instead of one master who could make her melt with barely a touch, she had two, although despite the intensity of the pleasure Mbweni had forced upon her she still loathed the woman. Mbweni was an unbearably smug, arrogant, nasty bitch.

Leah belonged to Morales, but Mbweni could do anything she wanted now, so long as he did not object. That infuriated Leah, for Mbweni liked nothing better than to taunt her and tease her, to make her feel degraded. And of course the woman was a lesbian, and a mean one. She had made no secret of her contempt for women who 'fucked' men. Mbweni was arrogantly proud to tell her that no man had ever fucked her, nor ever would.

'It seems two of the girls, the college girls, had their pictures in their college directory guide,' Scott went on. 'The firm that took the pictures also processed some for a private photographer who took images of the third girl during a publicity shoot. The picture that included her never ran in the paper, but it was in the database. We're narrowing our search now to anyone who had access to that database.'

'That can't be many people,' Leah said.

'No, pretty much those who worked there at any given time over the past couple of years. Trask is delighted. He sees the end of the case and the pressure he's under.'

'Yeah, I can imagine.'

'Odd how he asked for us, though. I mean, now he's narrowed the focus his own taskforce can handle the interviews and checks by themselves, so why bring us in on it?'

Because Mbweni told him to, Leah thought, though she didn't say. And Mbweni had done so because Morales told her to.

Morales knew something, knew more than he was saying, which would not be difficult as he said nothing. There were three girls missing, and Morales had had three girls for a long time – centuries, in fact. Was someone trying to imitate him to some degree? If so, did he have any idea who? Probably, but he wasn't telling the hired help.

The photography firm was not large. It was located in a modern, single-story office on the edge of town. It had an office staff of half a dozen, including the receptionist, financial clerks for billing, commercial salesmen and manager, and twelve photographers. Most of them seemed bewildered at the police attention.

Lieutenant Trask's team was focusing on several of the

photographers who seemed more than slightly defensive and hostile. Well, that breed tended to be anti-police and anti-establishment, Leah thought. Half of them probably did drugs as well.

It was not at all surprising they were looking mainly at the men, but Leah suspected that if the database was the link between the girls the person who had access to it was not the person who had caused the girls to disappear. No one with the kind of powers Morales had would stoop to actually working for a living.

She and Scott were not particularly welcomed, and were given the lower priority employees to interview, namely, the women. Again, the kind of questioning Scott led with was focused more on whom they might have incidentally provided access to. The men seemed to hold a kind of ingrained belief that a girl would not voluntarily be involved in such things, despite intellectually knowing better.

It was true that girls from good families with jobs rarely involved themselves in crime, but it did happen occasionally, usually at the behest of boyfriends. She let Scott ask the usual questions about boyfriends and histories, while she studied the girls. She was only vaguely aware that Morales was with her, noticing perhaps on an unconscious level as they interviewed a few of the girls.

But she became very much aware of his presence almost as soon as Allison Flemming sat down across from them. She understood his presence and his certainty that Flemming was involved, despite being shaken by the strength of his presence for a few moments, fighting to keep from showing it. But then as she focused on the girl she saw why.

She simply exuded sexuality.

And that was odd for she certainly didn't look like a sensual woman. She was nineteen, but she looked more like a virginal schoolgirl; wide-eyed, innocent, butter wouldn't melt in her mouth. She was petit, slim and blonde. Her hair was straight and fell below her shoulders, her eyes were sparkling and round, and she had a cute little nose.

Her attitude was one of earnestness and a straightforward desire to help. No, she had never used drugs of any kind, and highly disapproved of them. She had never been arrested, nor had she a boyfriend at the present time, nor within the last year.

And yet it was all a façade. Beneath she was, Leah somehow knew, sexually voracious even before someone had found her and marked her and made her even more a creature of sex. She lived alone with her cat, Sunshine, in a small apartment. She read a lot, and especially liked romance novels. No one would suspect her, and Leah could see that Scott was merely going through the motions. She could also see that she aroused him, though seemingly uncertain about why.

She ran through the excuses in her mind, considering how she could possibly justify further investigation into the girl, but nothing emerged from her thoughts. Scott would think she was mad. Trask would think her crazy and dismiss her out of hand.

Mbweni would devour this girl. Mbweni would adore her, not as a suspect but as dinner. And how would the girl react to Mbweni?

Nothing emerged from the interviews, though now all the employees would be further investigated, primarily the men, of course. And whoever looked into young Flemming would do so in a cursory manner and move on to something more likely.

'It's her,' Leah said.

Mbweni looked down at the photograph and then up again. 'You're kidding.'

Leah drew in a deep breath. 'She isn't as innocent as she appears.'

Mbweni smiled and reached out to cup Leah's breasts through her blouse. 'There's a lot of that going around. So you think she's like you, hmm?'

'I don't know. Maybe.'

Mbweni pinched her nipples possessively. 'Very well, you and Yi can look into her.'

'Sara?'

'Yes.' Mbweni smiled as she undid a few of the buttons of Leah's blouse and slipped her hand inside, and into her bra, feeling the stiff nipple poking firmly into her palm. 'I wish I could have her made as you,' she said thoughtfully. 'But then, with my newfound powers of sexual persuasion I suppose I scarcely need to.'

Then she drew back with a smile. 'The two of you can follow the little slut around after work and see what she gets up to.'

Leah started the car as she and Sara watched the girl trot down the street to the bus stop.

'You get on the bus with her,' Leah suggested. 'She knows me.'

Sara nodded and slipped out of the car, and Leah sighed with some relief as she left; the sexual tension in the car had been intense, the frustration miserable. Mbweni had given both of them a cruel dose of her sexual power before leaving. With a subdued Sara standing at her side she had kissed Leah and held her for long seconds as Leah's heart beat faster.

Then she did the same to Sara, and then with a smirk

she sent them out together to the car.

The bus came. It was crowded with rush-hour commuters, and Leah had no difficulty following as it made its slow way through the streets. She parked and waited, and her cell phone soon rang. Sara's voice was hushed and brief and informed her they were getting off the bus. She started the car and followed.

She picked up Sara as the two walked along the sidewalk. The girl was wearing sneakers, jeans, and a loose jacket. She went in through the wooden door of an older apartment building whose address matched the one she'd given the detectives as her home. Sara slipped into the car beside her, shaking her head.

'You should have seen her on the bus,' she said. 'She was flirting and fluttering her eyelashes at every male who looked her way, and that was plenty.'

'Interesting,' Leah mused.

'Frustrating,' Sara said with a scowl, and Leah understood at once. In her current condition Sara would have been intensely aroused by the sight.

Three quarters of an hour later the girl appeared again. Her hair was different, her make-up heavier, and she was wearing a short, tight black dress and high heels. They followed her to a club, and given the crowd Leah risked going in. The gyrating girl on the dance-floor was nothing like the sweet innocent they had interviewed. She was flaunting herself with a man outrageously, and his hands were all over her.

'Jeez,' Sara muttered, sipping a cola.

The couple disappeared through a back exit, and the two detectives hurried out the front then circled around, edging up to the alleyway, then pausing as they heard the passionate groans. They looked at each other, and then peeked around the corner.

Allison was bent over a garbage can, skirt hiked up, legs spread as the man she'd been dancing with thrust into her from behind. It was a brief but very vigorous bout, and her orgasm was vocal enough for the man to put a hand over her mouth to silence her as he completed his own business.

They then returned inside, and the two detectives followed.

'Little slut,' Sara muttered.

Allison abandoned her lover and found another man to dance with. There was no shortage of men eager for the opportunity.

'I think they know her here,' Leah said as she watched another man slip into the alley with the little blonde, who subsequently took six men into the alley during the course of the next two hours.

'You think she does this every night?' Leah asked, and Sara shrugged.

Finally the girl left in the company of two black men, and Leah and Sara followed them to a apartment a few miles away and waited outside.

'I think they're probably just chatting,' Leah said, and Sara sniffed in contempt.

An hour later a cab arrived and the girl emerged alone. They followed, but not to her own home. Instead she went to another club, where for the next two hours she danced, flirted, and led several men to a darkened corner near the toilets. The darkness and the pounding music blotted them out sufficiently for the patrons, who didn't much care anyway.

This time she left with three men, but only traveled as far as a nearby park, where she took all three on together, observed by Leah and Sara using infrared binoculars.

Afterwards they dropped her off at a scruffy bar. There she performed an amateur strip along with a half-dozen other girls, while the mainly male audience howled its approval. Then, partially clothed again, and supported by two men she apparently knew, she disappeared into a corner of the noisy bar. Leah and Sara couldn't make out what she was doing there, for the frames of many men blocked their view.

After a time Leah edged closer, and when no one was watching, pulled a wooden chair behind the crowd of men with their backs to her and got up onto it. She didn't need to look for long before jumping back down and returning to where Sara waited.

'She's naked and draped across a table, having sex with a couple of guys.'

'What a surprise. Do you suppose Mbweni has been kissing her lately?'

Leah pursed her lips. Neither had discussed the hunger each felt, and she wondered what Sara thought of the excitement Mbweni evoked in her. 'What do you mean?' she asked.

'I'm not sure,' Sara said. 'That woman sure can kiss, though. Well, you know what I'm talking about.' Leah nodded noncommittally. 'I felt my toes curl up. I swear I hate that bitch, but shit she can do awesome things to my body.'

Leah knew exactly what the girl was saying.

'You're not mad at me, are you?' Sara asked.

Leah blinked in surprise. 'Why?'

'You know.'

'Oh, no, it wasn't your fault,' Leah acknowledged. Sara had known, of course, about the hidden camera when she'd seduced Leah in her apartment, had known Mbweni would be observing. But Mbweni was a very powerful personality, even without her authority over Sara, even before she'd been equipped with the sexual power Morales had leant her. Sara, meanwhile, was merely a free spirit.

It was well over an hour before Allison stumbled out of the corner, dazed, bedraggled, but not looking terribly unhappy. She looked rather pleased with herself, in fact.

They followed her as she left the bar in company with an older man. The two parked for a time in a parking lot, and then the car drove off and left her on a street corner.

'Not another bar, I hope,' Leah sighed. But instead the girl walked only a short distance to a very stylish apartment building. She let herself in and the two quickly hurried up to the door, Sara grabbing it before it closed. Leah hung back lest the girl recognize her.

'She got into an elevator which went up to the penthouse,' Sara told her as she cautiously joined her.

The two got into an elevator but found it refused to travel to the top floor without a key. So they rode to the floor below it and got out, then went in search of the stairs.

The door to the top floor was locked, and they could hear nothing from within, but Leah felt Morales then, as if he were all around her, or inside her, and her hand reached out of its own accord and turned the knob, pulling the door open.

Sara stared. 'That was locked!'

'Maybe it wasn't closed tightly,' Leah suggested, knowing differently. She slipped inside, leaving Sara to follow, and they found themselves in a small lobby, the floor of pink marble, the walls of polished granite. There were two large doors before the elevator and Sara tried the handle, unsurprised to find it locked. They listened at the door.

'I think I hear her voice,' Leah said.

'And a man?'

The door abruptly opened and they both gasped and jerked back. A man stood there, tall, broad shouldered, with flowing blond hair – a veritable Norse god naked to the waist. Sara's eyes widened and Leah could see that she immediately fell under the man's influence. Leah felt it herself, felt the creeping admiration rising within her, but it was held in check by Morales' own hold on her.

The man smiled at them and Sara virtually melted against him. He reached out and took her hand, brushing his lips against the backs of her knuckles, and the wide-eyed girl fell slowly to her knees. Something told Leah that in addition to taking hold of her mind that touch told him everything she knew.

'Ah, a pair of police detectives,' he said. 'Do come in, my sweet dears.'

He took Leah's hand and she felt a jolt, but not, she thought, what Sara had felt. But still she fell to her knees, imitating Sara, wondering what the man would read from her, whether he would immediately realize she was Morales' tool. Those in the bar had noted at once that she'd been 'marked'. Surely this one would too.

Evidently not, for he drew them gently inside and then kissed them both, as Mbweni had done. But his lips and tongue had much more power, and both women felt their bodies become inflamed with passion as he led them into the apartment.

He led them through a large room centered around a shallow pool surrounded by colorful pillows and mats. A half dozen naked girls writhed on the pillows, and all began to beg for his attention as soon as he appeared. There were the three missing blonde girls, Leah thought dazedly, and three more besides that no one had reported missing.

They all looked like sisters, and were caressing each

other as they begged him to fuck them. But there was more, as if they were wearing odd costumes, costumes of white gold, costumes of fur… but not fur at all.

'In a moment, my dears,' he said.

Leah's breasts ached for his touch, her nipples already rigid. He held her arm firmly, leading her through the room and along a long hall to another. This room was oddly humid and brightly lit, like a greenhouse, and tall grass grew within. The man gave them a gentle shove and both girls, dazed and trembling, sprawled amid the grass.

At first, as Leah lay on her back, gasping, she thought the things around her were mushrooms, greenish and oddly tall, yet they were not. She tried to rise, only to find she couldn't, that her hair seemed caught in the grass, and then her hands were caught as well, and she could feel the grass actually moving, actually closing in around her, sliding up beneath her skirt and along her thighs, sliding into her sleeves and the neck of her blouse.

It was grass with a strength she had never known as she pulled against it helplessly, and felt it tugging up and back against her clothes. She felt the fabric tearing, parting, as the grass ripped through it. Alongside but out of her sight she could hear Sara moaning, could hear her clothes being torn.

But even as it did so she paid it only secondary attention. For the mushroom things, four or five inches high when she'd dropped among them, were growing and writhing and twisting around her and over her, now a foot tall, now two, and they no longer reminded her of mushrooms at all as they began to twine around her naked limbs, around her wrists and ankles, to snake their way along her arms and legs.

'Leah!'

'Sara?'

'W-what is this?' Sara gasped, tearing against the grass and mushrooms.

'I don't know.' She continued to struggle. Occasionally she would succeed in tearing one arm free, but only briefly, for another writhing tentacle, or mushroom, or whatever they were, would always wrap around it again. She was naked, the grass weaving around her.

She heard Sara cry out, but the cry was not of fear or pain. Leah twisted, gasping, and felt something moist and slick and warm against her bare sex, and tried to close her thighs.

She managed to pull her arm free of one of the things and turned over a little, then her arm was grasped again, this time by a thick green tube-like thing that twisted its way around her arm all the way to her shoulder.

She was pulled over onto her front, onto her hands and knees. She was partly covered in the things now, and strained helplessly against them as she felt a hot touch against her sex once more, felt a pressure against herself, of something soft yet firm pushing against her. 'No!' she gasped.

It twisted and turned and she felt her heart race, felt her senses sharpen as if they were fine-tuned, and then a wave of lust roared over her as the thing pushed wetly into her sex.

She cried out, a mixture of disgust, fear and excitement. She felt another pressing against her anus, twisting and pushing, seeking entry, and then something caught her nipples and jerked her attention down to where two more of the things, their mushroom heads opened wide, had closed entirely around each breast. She felt a squeezing, suckling sensation, and then cried out as another of the things thrust into her open mouth.

Disgust melted away as hunger and need blossomed,

and something at the back of her mind told her that whatever substance coated the tongues of Morales' little pets it was closely related to these things. Only here it was stronger – much stronger.

The fat green tubes writhed like snakes, slithering over her bare flesh, warm, slick with some kind of oozing fluid, yet very strong. Her mind was overcome by lust – literally. She had never felt such raw animal need, as if an impossibly powerful aphrodisiac had drugged her.

There was no room for fear in her mind, no place for worries or concern or anything else as wave after wave of intense bliss rolled through her. Her body began to undulate subconsciously in time with the snakelike tubes entwining around her.

It was as though she existed on a whole new plain of existence, a universe of sexual pleasure so intense it was almost unbearable. The tube within her pussy seemed to explode, to burst with a violence so powerful she could actually feel a steamy flood rushing into her womb, coating her insides as the tube deflated, then slid slowly back out of her aching sex and fell away.

Almost at once another thrust inside her, and she cried out at the force of it, cried out in bliss, her back arching as she was driven up and forward.

Then the one in her mouth also erupted, withdrawing as it did. She could feel the hot liquid pouring down into her belly, and coughed and choked as the thing slid back upward, the liquid thick and steaming, coating her throat then filling her mouth and overflowing. As the tube pulled free a final spurt of liquid poured over her face, as another tube drove straight into her gaping mouth and down her throat.

The things attached to her breasts were sucking painfully hard, but the pain brought only ecstasy as she writhed and twisted in the midst of the forest of snakes. Orgasm after orgasm sent her into helpless convulsions, her muscles spasming again and again.

She was barely capable of thought, even as another of the snakelike things emptied itself in her anus and was immediately replaced, was barely capable of caring about anything but the wondrous pleasure drowning her. She thought she might well die from such pleasure, but the thought was fleeting and drew no concern.

And indeed she would die, were it to continue. Already she was dazed, in a dreamlike state, soaked in the juices of the green tubes, her overheated body spasming as one tube after another poured its slippery fluids into and over her body.

Beside her Sara was in the same state as the green tubes swamped them. Neither was aware of the other, nor of anything else, dazed, overcome by the pleasure and wonder, choking and moaning around the tubes filling their mouths and throats as they shuddered to repeated climaxes as hour after hour slipped behind them.

Their exhaustion was soon total, yet the sexual heat continued to drive them on, well past their limits, their overloaded systems burning up as the intensity of the pleasure continued.

Neither noticed Morales as he stood at the entrance to the room, gazing dispassionately in at them.

He seemed to smile faintly, then slowly waved his hands over the teeming mass of greenery. In response the grass stilled, the snakelike tubes slowly sinking back into the floor.

The two girls were left lying exhausted, gasping for breath, trembling and shaking and moaning, nearly catatonic. As one their hands moved between their legs, fingers rubbing feverishly, bodies still driven on by the need and hunger filling them.

Another wave of Morales' hand, however, and the two stilled as well, losing consciousness. He turned away then, for he had other business to deal with.

Chapter Sixteen

Leah woke very slowly. For long minutes she drifted in and out of sleep, her mind never quite reaching a level that would allow to her think on anything but the most primitive levels of comfort, warmth and exhaustion.

And hunger, and thirst. She drank almost subconsciously, not entirely aware of how or what. Someone was there, someone who held a tube to her mouth, a tube through which pleasant tasting liquid could be sucked down her throat to ease some of her discomfort and allow her to again sink into comfortable sleep.

When finally her mind did awaken fully it was to a desire to remain where she was forever. The bed was extremely snug, and she was utterly drained. Every movement made her groan as if her battered body had been driven beyond its limits, every tired muscle ached.

She noted the figure that moved to the side of the bed, and she was now awake enough to wonder about it as a tube was held to her lips. She sucked in a cool, strawberry-flavored liquid, gazing at the person sitting on the edge of the bed holding it.

It was one of the blonde girls. The face was unmistakable, though not quite the same as the faces that had stared up from so many pictures over the previous weeks. The hair was thicker, longer, and more golden. It framed her face and swept her shoulders, highlighting jade-green eyes, a curved mouth, a snub nose and a rounded chin. There was something subtly different about the face than those she'd looked at before, and it was only when she noticed the girl's oddly pointed ears that she sensed what it was; the girl's features were feline.

Indeed, the girl's body was now discolored, matching her hair, and with fine soft lines that made her think immediately of layers of fur. It was as if the girl had been tattooed from neck to toe; yet somehow Leah knew no ink was involved.

The girl was nude save for a complex gold star surrounding each nipple. The star was flat against the centre of each breast, made of intricate and delicately shaped layers of gold. Each star had a small hole in its centre through which the girl's pink nipples protruded, and a thin gold pin piercing those nipples which held the stars in place against her soft, full breasts.

Between the girl's legs was a similar piece of jewelry, this one an inverted triangle, again with a hollow centre through which the girl's clitoris protruded, pierced as her nipples by the gold pin. She wore bands around her wrists and ankles of a similar design, and a collar around her throat.

Yet her face was one of utter serenity. It was not the doe-like animal innocence of Morales' bald pets, but one of contentment and peace. She drew back, her movements catlike, and Leah watched her pad to the door, open it, and leave.

She groaned weakly then sat up, wincing with effort, until she was sitting with her feet on the floor, trying to work her body into readiness for the supreme effort of standing upright.

Just then Morales entered the room, flanked by a pair of the catlike girls smiling down at her. The girls, without speaking, sank to their knees on either side of him as he stood beside the bed, their serene smiles never leaving their nearly identical faces.

'Awake at last,' he said.

'How long have I slept?' she asked tentatively.

'About thirty hours.'

Leah looked up at him a little blankly. She was finding it hard to really care. She felt shell-shocked, washed out, worn out, not just physically but emotionally, spiritually.

'Your friend is still unconscious. She was far worse off than you. You have rather special resources to draw upon; she does not. Still, she will survive, though she will have to be drawn more deeply into our little secrets than most mortals. She should make a fine addition to my little stable of females, and I think she should find that not unpleasant given her voracious sexual appetites.'

Leah nodded, understanding. 'What about them?' she asked, barely able to gesture in the direction of the two kneeling girls.

'Aren't they pretty,' he stated with a mild smile down at the two. 'Lorenzo did a very good job on them. I confess it's better, in some ways, than what I did with my own pets. But he was a bit greedy, of course, and made too much noise. For that he had to be punished.' He smiled smugly.

'You should... let them go,' Leah said weakly.

Morales snorted. 'To be what? Freaks? Those marks on their bodies will not fade, you know, nor can they be removed. The marks on their minds are even more permanent.'

Leah looked at the girls, and they smiled back.

'There is in all women, I think, a nurturing side,' he continued, 'and Lorenzo built that up and blended it with a sexual edge which makes them nearly as insatiable as my own little pets. He also made them quite biddable... no, that's the wrong term. He gave them a sense of endless

227

contentment with whatever they were doing. I don't think they could be unhappy if they tried. Isn't that right, my pets?'

'Yes, master,' the girls said in unison, beaming their agreement.

'They're quite as intelligent as ever they were, and understand everything which has happened and even why they feel so happy, but of course they're quite comfortable with it.

'They delight even more in being helpful, and in giving pleasure to others in any way whatever. In a perfect world we could let them go and they'd be fine. Even in this world we could simply send them home and they'd be quite content. They'd be endlessly used and abused, of course, by those they encountered, but they'd be happy with that.

'But unfortunately the authorities would wonder at their new, ah, skin tone, not to mention the changes to their faces and ears, and a few other things which aren't readily noticeable to the eye. No, I've already found nice homes for several of our little kittens. They'll be quite happy, and their owners will be in my debt. The girls will make delightful companions.'

Leah did not bother trying to tell him people should not be handed out like pets. After all, she was something of a pet herself, although in truth, she admitted to herself, his hold over her was mainly sexual. 'And what about me?' she asked, sinking back onto her elbows with a groan.

'What about you?' he mused. 'Oh, well, I'm going to keep a couple of these darlings for myself and they can look after my older pets, so that relieves you of that task. On the other hand, I still find you an oddly pleasant companion, of sorts. Your impudence and irritable nature notwithstanding, I find you quite interesting. Not that I necessarily like people arguing with me, but let's just say that girls who agree with everything I say do lack a certain something.'

He sat down beside her and reached out to stroke her hair.

'Besides, your life would be terribly wearisome without me, don't you think?

'No,' she said obstinately.

He chuckled and let his fingers trace a circle around her nearest nipple. 'If I turned you back, took away the enhancements I have given your body, you would never again know the intensity of the pleasure you have known with me. Your every sexual experience afterwards would be dull and without value. Do you really want to experience sex as you once did, with little excitement and even less pleasure?'

'I liked sex before,' she said stubbornly.

'Like now?'

'Now you've turned me into a nympho.'

'No, no, my dear, it is only the intensity of the pleasure your body feels now that makes you want sex more and more. Remove that pleasure and you'd come to find sex boring, dull, pointless.'

'There's more to life than—'

'Pleasure?'

'Than sex.'

'So? Who is stopping you from doing whatever you want? Have I not given you permission to be a police officer if you so desire? You can even be a better one now. Your senses are more finely honed, you have more energy, and you can read people much better than you once could.'

'I shouldn't need your permission,' she said.

He sighed and took a light grip on her hair, easing her

head back, Leah still too weary to resist. 'My dear child,' he purred, 'everyone, every mortal, answers to someone. You should be grateful the one you answer to is as kindly as I.'

Leah went back to work. Sara took longer to recover, but she too soon returned to work, though she continued to be used by Mbweni for 'special assignments', mostly sexual in nature. She was quite successful in them, however, and Mbweni soon built a reputation for putting pimps and other similar lowlife in prison.

Leah's wardrobe changed over the following weeks and months. She resisted it, to some degree, but whenever her disagreements with Mbweni came to open defiance the black woman's tongue would turn her will to jelly in short order. The very short minis, shorter even than the tight blazers she wore, caused plenty of talk, but no one could argue with her success rate.

And if there was speculation about the highly sexual nature of her life it remained far short of reality, as none of her colleagues could imagine the kind of wildness and sensual intensity she experienced each night at the hands of Morales and his pets – and his friends.

That intensity had changed her, just as Morales had said, and there was no going back to her ordinary life of near chastity. And, in fact, sometimes she admitted to herself that she bitched at Morales and Mbweni as much out of pride and habit as any lack of desire to partake in their lewd games.

If she was going to live for a long, long time, as it seemed was her destiny, it was not such a very bad life to have.

More exciting titles available from Chimera

All **Chimera** titles are available from your local bookshop or newsagent, or direct from our mail order department. Please send your order with your credit card details, a cheque or postal order (made payable to *Chimera Publishing Ltd*) to: **Chimera Publishing Ltd., Readers' Services, PO Box 152, Waterlooville, Hants, PO8 9FS.** Or call our **24 hour telephone/fax credit card hotline: +44 (0)23 92 646062** (Visa, Mastercard, Switch, JCB and Solo only).

UK & BFPO - Aimed delivery within three working days.
·   A delivery charge of £3.00.
·   An item charge of £0.20 per item, up to a maximum of five items.
For example, a customer ordering two items from the site for delivery within the UK will be charged £3.00 delivery + £0.40 items charge, totalling a delivery charge of £3.40. The maximum delivery cost for a UK customer is £4.00. Therefore if you order more than five items for delivery within the UK you will not be charged more than a total of £4.00 for delivery.

Western Europe - Aimed delivery within five to ten working days.
·   A delivery charge of £3.00.
·   An item charge of £1.25 per item.
For example, a customer ordering two items from the site for delivery to W. Europe, will be charged £3.00 delivery + £2.50 items charge, totalling a delivery charge of £5.50.

USA - Aimed delivery within twelve to fifteen working days.
·   A delivery charge of £3.00.
·   An item charge of £2.00 per item.
For example, a customer ordering two items from the site for delivery to the USA, will be charged £3.00 delivery + £4.00 item charge, totalling a delivery charge of £7.00.

Rest of the World - Aimed delivery within fifteen to twenty-two working days.
·   A delivery charge of £3.00.
·   An item charge of £2.75 per item.
For example, a customer ordering two items from the site for delivery to the ROW, will be charged £3.00 delivery + £5.50 item charge, totalling a delivery charge of £8.50.

Chimera Publishing Ltd

PO Box 152
Waterlooville
Hants
PO8 9FS

www.chimerabooks.co.uk
info@chimerabooks.co.uk
www.chimera-freedating.com

***

Sales and Distribution in the USA and Canada

Client Distribution Services, Inc
193 Edwards Drive
Jackson
TN 38301
USA

***

Sales and Distribution in Australia

Dennis Jones & Associates Pty Ltd
19a Michellan Ct
Bayswater
Victoria
Australia 3153